"Shouldn't you girls, be sitting at a table?"

Logan asked.

"I suggested that we move to a place that's a little more comfortable," Sandra said.

Logan frowned at her quick reply. "I can't see that you'll get much done lying all over the floor."

"Can I talk to you a moment, Mr. Napier?"

Sandra walked past Logan to his office. Momentarily taken aback, he couldn't help but follow.

Sandra turned to face him. "I understand your concern about the girls. But I think I need to establish something right from the beginning. I'm their teacher and I'll decide on the teaching methods."

Logan scowled. "I guess I need to make something clear, too, Miss Bachman. I'm their guardian and I'm the one who hired you."

Sandra crossed her arms, as if ready to face him down. "That's correct. But you came to me, I didn't come to you. In order for me to do my job, I need you to just let me do it."

"And if I don't like your methods?"

"Then I guess you'll be teaching them on your own."

Books by Carolyne Aarsen

Love Inspired

Homecoming #24
Ever Faithful #33
A Bride at Last #51
The Cowboy's Bride #67
*A Family-Style Christmas #86
*A Mother at Heart #94
*A Family at Last #121
A Hero for Kelsey #133
Twin Blessings #149

*Stealing Home

CAROLYNE AARSEN

lives in Northern Alberta where she was born, raised and married and is currently half finished raising her family of four—if raising children is a job that's ever done.

Carolyne's writing has been honed between being a stay-at-home mother, housewife, foster mother, columnist and business partner with her husband in their cattle farm and logging business. Writing for Love Inspired has given her the chance to combine her love of romance writing with her love for the Lord.

Twin Blessings
Carolyne Aarsen

Published by Steeple Hill Books™

STEEPLE HILL BOOKS

Steeple
Hill™

ISBN 0-373-87156-2

TWIN BLESSINGS

Copyright © 2001 by Carolyne Aarsen

Visit us at www.steeplehill.com

Printed in U.S.A.

When I consider Your heavens, the work of Your fingers, the moon and the stars which You have set in place, what is man that You are mindful of him and the son of man that You care for him?

—*Psalms* 8:3, 4

To Richard and my kids.
Always helpful and supportive.
Always enthusiastic and encouraging.

Chapter One

The sun was directly overhead.

Logan's vehicle was headed south. Down the highway toward Cypress Hills—oasis on the Alberta prairie and vacation home of Logan Napier's grandfather and parents.

Logan Napier should have been happy. No, Logan Napier should have been euphoric.

Usually the drive through the wide-open grasslands of the prairies put a smile on his face. The tawny landscape, deceptively smooth, soothed away the jagged edges of city living. The quiet highways never ceased to work their peace on him, erasing the tension of driving in Calgary's busy traffic.

Usually, Logan Napier drove one-handed, leaning back, letting the warm wind and the open space work its magic as he drove with the top of his convertible down.

Today, however, his hands clenched the steering wheel of a minivan, his eyes glaring through his sunglasses at the road ahead. In his estimation a single man moving up in the world shouldn't be driving a minivan. Nor should a single man be contemplating seven different punishments for ten-year-old twin nieces. And his mother.

All three were supposed to be neatly ensconced in the cabin in the hills. He was supposed to be coming up for a two-week holiday, spending his time drawing up plans for a house for Mr. Jonserad of Jonserad Holdings. If he was successful, it had the potential to bring more work from Jonserad's company to his architecture partnership.

Instead his mother had just called. She was leaving for Alaska in a day. Then the tutor called telling him that she was quitting because she wasn't getting the support she needed from Logan's mother. Each phone call put another glitch in his well-laid plans.

He hadn't planned on this, he brooded, squinting against the heat waves that shimmered from the pavement as he rounded a bend. Logan hit the on button of the tape deck and was immediately assaulted by the rhythmic chanting of yet another boy band, which did nothing for his ill humor. Every area of his life had been invaded by his nieces from the first day they came into his home, orphaned when their parents died in a boating accident.

Grimacing, Logan ejected the tape and fiddled with the dials. How was he supposed to work on this very important project with the girls around, unsupervised and running free?

How were they supposed to move on to the next grade if they didn't have a tutor to work with them?

And where was he supposed to find someone on such short notice? It had taken him a number of weeks to find one who was willing to go with the girls to Cypress Hills and to follow the studies their previous teacher had set out.

Glancing down, Logan gave the dial another quick twist. Finally some decent music drifted out of the speakers. He adjusted the tuner then glanced up.

He was heading directly toward a woman standing on the side of the road.

Logan yanked on the steering wheel. The tires squealed on the warm pavement as the van swung around her.

He slammed on the brakes. The van rocked to a halt, and Logan pulled his shaking hands over his face.

He took a slow breath and sent up a heartfelt prayer, thankful that nothing more serious had happened. He got out of the van in time to see the woman bearing down on him, a knapsack flung over one shoulder.

Her long brown hair streamed behind her, her eyes narrowed.

"You could have killed me," she called, throwing her hands in the air.

"I'm sorry," he said, walking toward her. "Are you okay?"

"I'm fine. You missed me." She stopped in front of him, her hands on her hips, her dark eyes assessing him even as he did her.

She was of medium height. Thick brown hair hung in a heavy swath over one shoulder. Her deep brown eyes were framed by eyebrows that winged ever so slightly, giving her a mischievous look. Her tank top revealed tanned arms, her khaki shorts long, tanned legs. Bare feet in sandals. Attractive in a homegrown way.

"What were you doing?" she asked.

Logan blinked, realizing he was studying her a little too long. Chalk it up to loneliness, he thought. And he must be lonely if he was eyeing hitchhikers. "Just trying to find a radio station," he said finally.

She shook her head, lifting her hair from the back of her neck. "Checking the latest stock quotations?"

In spite of the fact that he knew he hadn't been paying attention and had almost missed her, Logan still bristled at her tone. "Why were you on the side of the road?" he returned.

A few vehicles whizzed by, swirling warm air around the two of them.

"Thumbing for a ride." She let her hair drop, tilted her head and looked past him. "I suppose you'll have to give me one now, since you've almost killed me and then made me miss a few potentials."

She didn't look much older than twenty and about as responsible as his nieces. He wasn't in the mood to have her as a passenger, but he did feel he owed her a ride.

"I didn't almost kill you," he said, defending himself. "But I am sorry about the scare."

"So do I get a ride?"

Logan hesitated. He felt he should, though he never picked up hitchhikers as a rule.

"I won't kill you, if that's what you're worried about." Her lips curved into a smirk. "And I won't take your wife and kids hostage or try to sue you for taking five years off my life.''

''I don't have a wife and kids.''

''But you have a minivan.''

Logan frowned at her smirk and decided to let the comment pass. He wasn't in the mood to defend the necessity of his vehicle to a complete stranger, not with the sun's heat pressing all around. ''Look, I'm sorry again about what I did. But I'm running late. If you want a ride, I'm leaving now.''

He didn't look to see if she had followed him, but she had the passenger door open the same time he had his open.

''Nice and cool in here,'' she said, pulling off her knapsack. She dropped it on the floor in front of her and looked around. ''So, what's a guy like you need a minivan for?'' she asked, as Logan clicked his seat belt shut.

''What do you mean, a guy like me?'' Logan frowned as he slipped on his sunglasses and checked his side mirror.

''Near as I can see, I figure you for an accountant,'' she said, glancing around the interior of the van. ''Laptop in the seat, briefcase beside it. All nice and orderly. Someone like you should be driving a sedan, not a van.''

''Do you usually analyze the people who pick you up?'' Logan asked as he pulled onto the road, regretting his momentary lapse that put him in this predicament. He had things on his mind and didn't feel like listening to meaningless chatter.

"I need to. I hear too many scary stories about disappearing women."

"So why take the chance?" He glanced at her, and in spite of his impression of her, he was struck once again by her straightforward good looks.

"Sense of adventure. The lure of the open road." She shrugged. "That and the free ride."

"Of course."

"Okay, I detect a faint note of derision in your voice," she said with a light laugh. "If you're an accountant, I would imagine that there isn't a column in your life for freeloaders."

Logan didn't deign to answer that one.

She waited, then with a shrug bent over and pulled a bottle of water out of her knapsack. Twisting off the top, she offered some to him. "Some free water as payment for my free ride?"

He shook his head.

The woman took a sip and backhanded her mouth. Out of the corner of his eye he could see her scrutiny.

"To further answer your previous question about taking chances," she continued. "I have to admit that I don't see you as a threat."

Logan only nodded, unwilling to encourage her. He didn't really want to talk. He preferred to concentrate on his most recent problem.

"You've got the briefcase, which could be hiding a murder weapon," she said, as if unaware of his silence, "but I'm sure if I were to open it, it would be full of paper. Probably the financial section of the newspaper, folded open to the stock market. Let's see, what else," she mused aloud, still studying him. "A calculator, some sort of computerized personal organizer, a variety of pens and pencils, a package of chewing gum, a manual of one type or another and business cards, of course. Lots of business cards. Murderers don't usually carry that kind of thing. But my biggest clue that you're not a murderer is this.'' She held up the tape that had fallen out of the tape deck. "I don't think boy bands singing 'oh baby, baby, you are a little baby, you baby' is what a would-be murderer would listen to.'' She stopped finally, turning the tape over in her hands. "Of course, listening to it might drive you to murder.''

In spite of the minor annoyance of her chatter, Logan couldn't stop the faint grin teasing his mouth at her last statement.

"Ah, Mr. Phlegmatic does have a faint sense of humor,'' she said, lifting her bare feet to the seat and clasping her arms around her knees.

"This Mr. Phlegmatic would prefer it if you buckled up,'' he said finally.

"And Mr. P. talks,'' she said with a saucy grin. But to his surprise she lowered her feet and obediently buckled up. "So what do you do when you're not running over women on the side of the road?''

Logan shook his head in exasperation. "Look, I already apologized for that,'' he said with a measure of asperity. "I don't make a habit of that anymore than I make a habit of picking up hitchhikers.''

"Well, for that I'm grateful. And of course, very grateful that I don't have to worry about not reaching my destination.''

"And where, ultimately, is that?'' he asked.

"The next stop on this road," the woman said with a laugh. "The Hills."

"That's where I'm headed, too."

"That's just excellent." She beamed at him, and Logan felt a faint stirring of reaction to her infectious enthusiasm.

He pulled himself up short. This woman was definitely not his type, no matter how attractive she might be. He put his reaction down to a melancholy that had been his companion since he and Karen had broken up.

A gentle ache turned through him as he thought of Karen. When Logan was awarded sole guardianship of his nieces, Karen had decided that the responsibility was more than she could handle. So she broke up with Logan. At the time he didn't know if it was his pride or his feelings that hurt more. He still wasn't sure.

"So what's your name?" he asked, relegating that subject to the closed file.

"Sandra Bachman. Pleased to make your acquaintance, Mr. P."

Logan decided to leave it at that. He wasn't as comfortable handing out his name. Not to a total stranger.

She smiled at him and looked at the countryside. "Do you come here often?"

Logan glanced sidelong at her, realizing that she wasn't going to be quiet. Ignoring her didn't work, so he really had not choice but to respond to her. "Not as often as I'd like," he admitted. "I work in Calgary."

"As an accountant?"

"No. Architect."

"Ooh. All those nice straight lines."

Logan ignored her slightly sarcastic remark. "So what do you do?"

Sandra lay her head back against the headrest of the car. "Whatever comes to mind. Wherever I happen to be." She tossed him another mischievous glance. "I've been a short-order cook on Vancouver Island, a waitress in California, a receptionist in Minnesota. I've worked on a road crew and tried planting trees." She wrinkled her nose. "Too hard. The only constant in my life has been my stained glass work."

"As in church windows?"

"Sometimes. Though I don't often see the finished project."

"Why not?"

"Been there, done that and bought the T-shirt. Not my style."

Sandra Bachman sounded exactly like his mother— always moving and resistant to organized religion.

"Do you go to church?" she asked.

"Yes, I do," he said hoping that his conviction came through the three words. "I attend regularly."

"Out of need or custom?"

He shook his head as he smiled. "Need is probably uppermost."

"A good man." Again the slightly sarcastic tone. In spite of his faint animosity toward her, he couldn't help but wonder what caused it.

"Going to church doesn't make anyone good anymore than living in a garage makes someone a mechanic," he retorted.

She laughed again, a throaty sound full of humor. "Good point, Mr. P."

She tilted her head to one side, twisting her hair around her hand. "You have a cabin in Elkwater?"

Logan nodded, checking his speed. "It's my grandfather's."

"So you're on holiday."

"Not really."

"Okay, you sound defensive."

"You sound nosy."

Sandra laughed. "You're not the first one to tell me that." She gave her hair another twist. "So if you're not on holiday, why are you going to a holiday place?"

"I have to meet my mother." *And try and talk some sense into her,* Logan thought. If he could convince his mother to stay, he might win a reprieve.

"So she's holidaying."

Logan glanced at Sandra, slightly annoyed at her steady probing. "My mother has her own strange and irresponsible plans," he said.

His passenger angled him a mischievous glance, unfazed by his abrupt comments. "I sense tension between your mother's choice of lifestyle and yours."

"That's putting it kindly. My mother has a hard time with responsibility."

"Surely you're being a little hard on her? After all, she raised you, didn't she?"

Logan held her dancing eyes, momentarily unable to look away, catching a glimmer of her enthusiasm. She tilted her head again, as if studying him, her smile fading.

Her expression became serious as the contact lengthened.

She really was quite pretty, Logan thought. Possessed an infectious charm.

He caught himself and looked at the road, derailing that particular train of thought. This young woman was as far from what he was looking for as his mother was.

"So why are you so defensive about your mother?"

"Why do you care? I'll probably never see you again."

She lifted her shoulder in a negligent shrug. "Just making conversation. We don't need to talk about your mother," Sandra continued, biting her lip as if considering a safe topic. "We could talk about life, that one great miracle."

"Big topic."

"Depends on how you break it down." She twirled a loose strand of hair around her finger. "What do you want from life?"

Logan wasn't going to answer, but he hadn't spent time with an attractive woman since Karen. He found himself saying, "Normal. I yearn for absolutely normal." He wasn't usually this loquacious with a complete stranger and wondered what it was about her that had drawn that admission from him.

"Normal isn't really normal, you know," Sandra replied, braiding her hair into a thick, dark braid. Her dark eyes held his a brief moment. "Sometimes normal makes you crazy."

Logan gave her a quick look. "Now you sound defensive."

"Nope. Just telling the truth." She dropped the braid, and it lay like a thick rope over her tanned shoulders. "So what's your plan to get your normal life?"

"That's an easy one. I'm picking up my nieces, who are staying with my mother, who wants to scoot off to Alaska for some strange reason. Then I'm taking my nieces back home to Calgary. And that's as close to normal as I'm going to get."

The woman's smile slipped, and she looked straight ahead. "Nieces?" she asked quietly. "As in two?"

"A matched set," Logan replied. "Twin girls that have been a mixed blessing to me."

She tossed him a quick glance, then looked away, as if retreating. She folded her hands on her lap, lay her head against the backrest and closed her eyes. The conversation had come to an end.

Logan wondered what caused the sudden change this time. Wondered why it bothered him. Wondered why he should care.

He had enough on his mind. He concentrated on the road, watching the enticing oasis of Cypress Hills grow larger, bringing Logan closer to his destination and decisions.

Finally the road made one final turn and then skirted the lake for which the town of Elkwater was named. Sandra sat up as Logan slowed down by the town limits.

"Just drop me off at the service station," Sandra said.

He pulled up in front of the confectionary and gas station and before he could get out, Sandra had grabbed her backpack and was out of the van.

"Thanks for the ride, Mr. P.," she said with a quick grin. "I just might see you around."

Logan nodded, feeling suddenly self-conscious at all

that he had told her, a complete stranger. He wasn't usually that forthcoming. "You're welcome," he said automatically. She flashed him another bright smile then jogged across the street.

Logan slowly put the car in gear, still watching Sandra as she greeted a group of people standing by the gas pumps, talking. She stopped.

Logan couldn't hear what she was saying but could tell from her gestures that she was relating her adventures of the day. They laughed, she laughed and for a moment Logan was gripped by the same feeling he had when she had first smiled at him.

He pulled away, shaking his head at his own lapse, putting it down to his frustration and, if he were to be honest, a measure of loneliness. Sandra Bachman was a strange, wild young woman, and he'd probably never see her again.

A few minutes later he pulled in beside a small blue car parked in front of a large A-frame house with a commanding view of Elkwater Lake.

"Oh, Logan, my darling. There you are." Florence Napier stood on the porch of the house, her arms held out toward her only son.

As he stepped out of the car to greet his mother, Logan forced a smile to his lips at his mother's effusive welcome. It always struck him as false, considering that when he and his sister were growing up, Florence Napier seldom paid them as much attention as she did her current project.

"Come and give us a kiss," she cried. Today she wore a long dress made of unbleached cotton, covered with a loosely woven vest. Her long gray hair hung loose, tangling in her feathered earrings.

Her artistic pose, Logan thought as he dutifully made his way up the wooden steps to give her a perfunctory hug.

"I'm so glad you came so quickly, Logan. I was just packing up to leave." Florence tucked Logan's arm under hers and led him into the house. "I got an unexpected call from my friend Larissa. You remember her? We took a charcoal class together when we lived in Portland. Anyhow, she's up in Anchorage and absolutely begged me to join her. She wants to do some painting. Of course I couldn't miss this opportunity. We're hoping to check out Whitehorse and possibly Yellowknife, since we're up there anyway."

Logan didn't care to hear about his mother's itinerary. He knew from his youth how hectic it would be. He had more important things to deal with. "Where are Brittany and Bethany?"

Florence wrinkled her nose. "Upstairs. Pouting. I told them you would be taking them home since that dyspeptic tutor you hired decided to quit." Florence shrugged, signifying her inability to understand the tutor's sudden flight.

"Diane has left already?" Logan had to ask, was hoping and praying it wasn't true.

Florence's shoulders lifted in an exaggerated sigh. "Yes. Two days ago. I've never seen a woman so lugubrious."

Logan pulled his arm free from his mother, glaring at her, his frustration and anger coming to the fore. "I talked to her when she phoned me. She told me that you never backed her decisions.''

Florence looked at him, her fingertips pressed to her chest. "Logan. That woman's goal was to turn my granddaughters into clones of herself.''

"Considering that she came very well qualified, that might not have done Bethany and Brittany any harm.''

Logan's mother tut-tutted. "Logan, be reasonable. They're young. It's July. They shouldn't have to do schoolwork. I moved you and your sister all over the country, and it never did you any harm.''

"Not by your standards,'' Logan retorted. For a moment he was clearly reminded of Sandra.

Lord, give me strength, give me patience, he prayed. *Right now would be nice.* "They were also both earning a 45% average in school,'' Logan said, struggling to keep his tone even. "It was only by begging and agreeing to hire a tutor to work with them over the summer that they won't have to repeat grade five. If they don't finish the work the teacher sent out and if they don't pass the tests she's going to give them at the end of the summer, they will repeat grade five.''

A quick wave of Florence's hand relegated his heated remarks to oblivion. At least in her estimation. "My goodness, Logan. You put too much emphasis on formal education.'' Then she smiled at him. "But don't worry. I'm fully cognizant of your plans and I've already had the good luck and foresight to find a tutor for the girls. Imagine. She lives right here in Elkwater.''

"Really? And what are her qualifications?'' Logan was almost afraid to ask.

"She has a Bachelor of Education from a well-respected eastern university. With—" she raised an index finger as if to drive her point home "—a major in history."

"And what is this paragon's name?"

"Sandra. Sandra Bachman."

So now what are you going to do? Sandra thought, dropping her knapsack on her tiny kitchen table. She pushed her hair from her face and blew out her breath in a gusty sigh.

She was pretty sure the man who had just dropped her off was the same Uncle Logan that Bethany and Brittany were always talking about. After all, what were the chances of two men having twin nieces living in Elkwater?

From the way the girls spoke of him she had pictured the mysterious uncle to be a portly gentleman, about sixty years old, with no sense of humor.

The real Uncle Logan was a much different story. Tall, thick dark hair that held a soft wave, eyebrows that could frown anyone into the next dimension, hazel eyes fringed with lashes that put hers to shame. His straight mouth and square jaw offset his feminine features big time.

The real Uncle Logan was a dangerous package, she thought. Dangerously good-looking, if one's tastes ran to clean-cut corporate citizens like accountants. Architects, she corrected. She knew from the girls that Uncle Logan was an architect. She bet he had a closet full of suits at home.

Sandra shuddered at the thought. Her tastes never

ran in that direction. If anything, they went in the complete opposite direction of anyone remotely like her father, the epitome of conventional and normal that Logan wanted so badly.

Suppressing a sigh, Sandra slipped into the tiny bedroom and quickly changed into the clothes she had planned to wear for her third and what could possibly be final day on the job. She was tempted to stay away, knowing that losing her job was inevitable, given the way Logan was talking in the car on the way up here, but she had made a deal with Florence Napier. And Sandra held the faint hope that Florence might come through for her.

The walk to the Napier cabin only took ten minutes, but with each step Sandra wondered at the implications for her future. She needed this job to pay for the shipment of glass that would only be delivered cash on delivery. Trouble was she only had enough cash for a few groceries and not near enough for the glass.

At one time she'd been a praying person, but she didn't think God could be bothered with something as minor as a desperate need for money to pay bills.

As she rounded the corner, she saw Logan's van parked beside Florence's car, and her step faltered as she remembered what the girls had told her about Uncle Logan.

A tough disciplinarian who made them go to church every Sunday whether they wanted to or not. A man who kept them to a strict and rigid schedule.

A shiver of apprehension trailed down Sandra's neck at the thought of facing Logan again. This time as her potential boss. A boss she had smart mouthed on the way here. Why had she done it? she thought.

Because he was just like her father, she reminded herself. Though Sandra knew she would never dare be as flippant with Josh Bachman as she was with the formidable Logan Napier.

The front door of the cabin opened, and Florence stepped out carrying a garment bag. She lifted her head at the same moment Sandra stepped forward.

"Oh, Sandra. Hello, darling. We've been waiting for you." Florence set the garment bag on the hood of her little car and flowed toward Sandra, enveloping her in a hug. "The girls were wondering if you were even coming today."

"I'm sorry." Sandra made a futile gesture in the direction of Medicine Hat. "My car. I brought it in for a routine oil change but they found more trouble with it."

"Goodness, how did you get here?"

Sandra caught her lip between her teeth as she glanced at Logan's minivan. "I hitchhiked."

"That's my girl," Florence said approvingly. "Innovative and not scared to accept a challenge." Florence smiled, but Sandra sensed a measure of hesitation.

"So, where are the girls?" Sandra didn't know her status, but she figured it was better to simply act as if she still had a job.

Florence laid an arm over Sandra's shoulders, drawing her a short distance away from the house. "There's been a small complication, Sandra," Florence said, lowering her voice. "The girls' uncle came here. Unexpectedly.'' Florence laughed as if dismissing this minor problem.

Sandra gave her a weak smile in return. ''And what does that mean?'' As if she didn't know. Staid Uncle Logan would hardly approve of a smart-mouthed hitchhiking tutor, regardless of her reasons.

''I think we're okay, but you will have to talk to him.''

''Haven't you talked to him yet? Haven't you told him that you hired me? We had an agreement.''

Florence tossed a furtive glance over her shoulder, and that insignificant gesture told Sandra precisely how much influence Florence had with Uncle Logan.

None.

Florence looked at Sandra, her hand resting on Sandra's shoulder. ''It would probably be best if you spoke with him. Told him your credentials, that kind of thing.''

Sandra looked at Florence, whose gaze flittered away. ''Okay. I will. Where is he?''

''He's in the house. He's unpacking, so I think that means he'll be staying at least tonight.'' Florence turned, giving Sandra a light push in the direction of the house. ''You go talk to him. You'll do fine.''

''Thanks for the vote of confidence,'' Sandra muttered as she faced the house. She took a deep breath and walked purposefully toward the cabin. Up the stairs, her footsteps echoing on the wood, and then she was standing at the door.

She knocked, hesitant at first, then angry with her indecisiveness, knocking harder the second time.

The door opened almost immediately, making Sandra wonder if he had been watching to see if she would come to the house.

Logan stood framed by the open door. He looked as conservative as he had when he picked her up. Khaki pants, a cotton button-down shirt. All he was missing was a pair of glasses and a pocket protector.

"Hi," she said with a forced jocularity. "You know who I am. Now you know what I am."

Logan wasn't smiling, however. "Come on in, Sandra. We need to talk."

Sandra knew that though she may have weaseled a smile out of him this afternoon, she probably wouldn't now.

Chapter Two

~❧~

As Sandra walked past him, Logan caught his mother's concerned look. But Florence stayed where she was.

He wasn't surprised that his mother didn't come rushing in to support the person she had hired. Confrontation wasn't Florence's style.

Logan closed the door quietly and turned to face Sandra. She wore a dress with short sleeves. Demure and much more suited to a teacher than the shorts and tank top she had on this afternoon. She had tied up her hair earlier into some kind of braid, finishing the picture.

"Are the girls around?" Sandra asked, her hands clasped in front of her.

"They're upstairs, I think. They haven't dared to come down yet." Logan rested his hands on his hips as he studied her. She was as pretty as before, but definitely not the type of girl he wanted teaching his flighty nieces. They needed an older, stronger influence.

"Do I pass?" she asked suddenly, her brown eyes narrowed.

Logan held her gaze. "I'm sorry to tell you this, Sandra, but you don't have a job. The girls and I are heading back to Calgary tomorrow."

"I thought they were staying here for the summer."

"They were." Logan put emphasis on the last word. "But their antics and those of my mother have proved to me that they are better off in Calgary where I can keep a close eye on them." It wasn't what he wanted at all, but he certainly wasn't going to leave them with someone like her.

"Your mother hired me to teach the girls for the rest of the summer. We had an agreement."

Logan heard the contentious tone in her voice but wasn't moved by it. "I'm the legal guardian of these girls, and I'm the one who has to make decisions that I think are best for them. Not my mother."

"And you wouldn't consider letting the girls stay and having me tutor them?"

Logan shook his head. His nieces had spent enough of their life living around unsuitable people when their parents were alive, carting them around from boat race to boat race. It had taken him a couple of months just to get them into a normal household routine, let alone a schoolwork one. The last thing he wanted was for all his careful and loving work to be undone by someone whose character he knew precious little of. A woman whose first impression was hardly stellar.

"So you're dismissing me out of hand." Her voice

rose ever so slightly. "Without even considering my credentials as a teacher."

"What references do you have? Have you ever worked as a teacher since you graduated?"

"No, I haven't."

"So what have you done?"

Sandra said nothing, and Logan couldn't help but remember her casual comments about work as they had driven here.

"I'm sorry, Sandra," he said. "I have to make a judgment call in this situation."

"Does this have anything to do with the fact that I was hitchhiking this afternoon?"

Logan didn't know what to say. Should he tell an untruth or be bluntly honest?

She laughed shortly. "I can't believe this. I'm perfectly qualified...." She let the sentence slide off.

Logan's shoulders lifted in a sigh as he shoved his hands in the pockets of his pants. "I didn't interview you, Sandra. I had chosen another eminently qualified tutor..."

"I have a Bachelor of Education degree," Sandra stated. "With a major in history and a minor in English. Nothing wrong with that, I'm sure."

Logan bristled at her tone. "I have my nieces' well-being to consider, besides their education."

Sandra held his steady gaze, then her eyes drifted away. "I see." She darted another angry look his way. "Then I'll be on my way." She strode past him and out of the house.

Logan watched her go, fighting a moment's panic. It would solve so many things if he were to let the girls stay with Sandra. He was in the middle of a hugely important project and he needed all the free time he could get.

But common sense made him keep his mouth shut. Common sense and an innate concern for his nieces. They needed stability and a firm hand. Something that had been sorely lacking in their life.

And, when he was younger, his own.

Logan spent his teen years moving from school to school, dragged across the country by parents searching for the elusive perfect job.

Education wasn't taken seriously in this branch of the Napier family, and as a consequence Logan and his sister Linda's schooling suffered. Always behind academically, Logan dedicated every spare moment to catching up, to striving to get out of the rut his parents seemed willing to flow along in. Then, when Logan was in high school, his father died and Florence Napier was forced to settle down for a while.

During this time Logan pulled himself out of the endless routine of constant movement. He applied himself to finishing high school and going to college. Six years ago he graduated with his degree and was much happier than he had ever been during his aimless childhood.

However, Linda, the twins' mother, had been caught up in the same ceaseless wandering, hooking up and marrying a man who raced speedboats for thrills and the occasional cash prize. An aquatic cowboy who didn't know where his own parents were. Brittany and Bethany were headed in the same direction until a tragic accident claimed Logan's sister and her husband's life. To his mother's surprise Logan had been named not only guardian but also executor of the small estate the girls had inherited.

Bethany and Brittany's arrival changed everything in Logan's life, but he was determined to do right by them. To take care of them. To make sure that any influence in their life was positive and stable.

A young woman like Sandra Bachman was not the kind of person he wanted tutoring these impressionable young girls.

With a sigh and another quick prayer, he turned to the next task at hand.

"Okay, girls. You can stop listening in and come down."

Two heads popped above the blanket draped over the balustrade of the loft. Both blond, both cute, both looking slightly chastened.

Brittany, the bolder of the two, bounced down the stairs as only a young girl could and landed in front of him, her hands tucked in the pockets of her very baggy white pants. Bethany followed a few paces behind, looking a little more subdued than her counterpart.

Brittany lifted her shoulders, looking genuinely puzzled. "So I guess you came here earlier than you figured. Are you sure you don't want to stay for a while?"

Logan shook his head slowly, as if for emphasis. "I have a special project I need to work on. You know work? The thing that keeps you in those ridiculous clothes?" He pressed his lips together, frustrated at the anger that had surged to the fore. But today had not been a good day, and right now he was all out of magical patience.

Brittany slowly tilted her head as if searching for some kind of answer.

Logan didn't wait for her to find it. "You and Bethany had better hustle yourselves back upstairs and start packing. We're leaving for Calgary tomorrow."

"What?" The word spilled out of both girls' mouths at the same time.

"We can't go now... You promised... You said we'd stay here all summer." Their sentences tumbled over and through each other.

"We've only been here a couple of weeks," Bethany wailed.

Logan glanced at the more docile of the pair, and he felt the hard edges of his anger blur. "Sorry, hon. You guys had your chance and you blew it. We're going back."

"We didn't know it was a test," Brittany cried, her blue eyes glistening.

"It wasn't a test," Logan growled, trying manfully to face down the tears that spilled down both their cheeks. "I don't want to stay here, your grandmother has decided to chase some dream, and you chased off your last tutor, so you have to come back with me."

"But why can't Sandra teach us?" Bethany sniffed, wiping away her tears with the back of her hand. She sat down on the lowest step, still sniffling.

Logan sighed, plowing his hand through his hair. He could feel himself wavering and knew he shouldn't. He could deal with upstart contractors and rude co-workers, but his nieces' tears always unmanned him.

"Because I don't think she is capable. That's why."

"But we had hoped to stay. We haven't been here

since Mom and Dad…'' Brittany's voice broke, and she sat beside her sister, pressing her hands against her face, unable to finish.

Logan's heart melted completely. It had been eighteen months since the girls' parents were killed. This summer was the first time they had come back to this place where they and their parents would often stop by on their way to the next destination. It was one of the few constants in their childhood.

It had been difficult enough for him to lose his sister. He couldn't imagine how hard it was for them to lose both parents. And now he was going to take them away from the one place they had fond memories of.

He sat on the step between the girls and put his arms awkwardly around their narrow shoulders. "Oh, sweeties," he said, stroking their arms, wishing he knew exactly what to say. Brittany leaned against him, sniffing loudly.

"Can we stay just for a little while?" Brittany murmured.

Logan considered his options as he drew her close. He had counted on staying here and working for a couple of weeks anyhow. It would take at least a couple of days to find another tutor, even if he did leave tomorrow. Which meant he would be stuck with two cranky girls in a condo in Calgary.

Hold your ground, he reminded himself. *Don't let them think all they have to do is cry and they can get their way.*

But while the rational part of his mind argued the point, his shirt was getting damp from his nieces' tears. Tears that he knew were genuine.

"I suppose we could stay here for a little while." He relented, ignoring a riffle of panic. He had three weeks to brainstorm an idea for a house, do a drawing and create blueprints, then another week to build a model of the idea.

The biggest hitch in all of this was that he didn't have an idea.

You don't have time for this, the sane part of his mind said.

"For a little while? Really?" Bethany lifted her head as a tear slid silently down her cheek.

Logan sighed, bent over and dropped a light kiss on her head. "Yes, really."

He was rewarded with a feeble smile.

"Thank you, Uncle Logan," Bethany said, wiping her cheeks as she sat up.

"But I need your help." He tried to sound stern. "No fooling around. Just do what I ask."

"So that means no schoolwork?" Brittany asked.

Logan sighed. "No. It means I'll have to help you with it until we get back to Calgary. I'm going to start looking for a tutor right away."

Brittany's face fell. "And what about Sandra?"

"I told you already, she is not teaching you. And I'm not going to talk about it while we're here."

He almost missed the glint in Bethany's eye as she glanced at her sister. But as she looked at him, her blue eyes guileless as ever, he figured he must have imagined it.

"And there's no way I could get an advance from you?" Sandra bit her lip as she heard what she knew she would. The restaurant would absolutely not give her a dime until she delivered twenty lamps as promised. She knew that, but thought she would give it a try. "Thanks, then. No, there's no problem. I have other resources," she lied. She hung up the phone.

"I'm not going to worry, I'm not going to worry," Sandra muttered as she grabbed her sweater and slipped it over her shoulders. Trouble was, try as she might, she couldn't stifle the panic that fluttered in her chest.

After months of work and inexpert marketing, she had gotten the first break with her stained glass work. A restaurant in Calgary had ordered twenty lampshades. If they liked her work, she had a good chance to make more for some of their other locations.

Trouble was she was desperately short of money. The unexpected move here from Saltspring Island in British Columbia had cut into her meager savings. She had one month's rent paid on the cabin, and Cora, her friend and roommate, was nowhere to be found.

Working for Florence Napier had been the blessing she had been looking for.

And now that was over, too. Her broken-down car wouldn't even allow her to work in Medicine Hat.

Sandra took a deep breath, then another, hoping the mad flutters in her heart would settle once she started on her usual evening walk.

Outside, the sun's penetrating warmth had softened and a faint breeze wafted off the lake.

Sandra paused, letting the evening quiet soothe her. Except it didn't.

She buttoned her sweater and started down the street

toward the boardwalk that edged the beach and followed the lake. Her steady tread on the boards echoed hollowly, creating a familiar rhythm.

What to do, what to do, what to do.

Phone home?

The thought slipped insidiously through her subconscious. She let it drift a moment, then pushed it ruthlessly aside.

Phone home and hear how useless she was? Phone home and hear, "Why don't you do anything constructive with that education degree I paid so much money for?"

Sandra shivered, even though it was warm. Conforming was the way things happened in her home. Conform and you get to come along on promised trips. Conform and your education will be paid for. Conform and Father would deign to talk to you. Sandra conformed, trying in vain to live up to the expectations of a father who was never satisfied. She got her degree, and as soon as she could, she fled. All the way to Vancouver Island.

Five years and a hundred experiences later, Sandra's flight from conformity had washed her up here, in Cypress Hills, a four-hour drive from where she started, flat broke with a roommate who had flittered off again.

The evening breeze picked up a little, riffling the water and teasing her hair. Sandra sucked in another breath and squared her shoulders. She wasn't going to give up. Not yet.

She ambled along the boardwalk, her arms wrapped around herself. Life was still good, she thought, raising her face to the unbearable blue of the Alberta sky. She was still alive and still free, and no one could put a price on that.

"Hey, Sandra."

Sandra lowered her head, wondering who had called her. She looked around and saw Bethany and Brittany sitting on a bench, swinging their legs.

"Hey, yourself." She walked over, happy to see these two very rambunctious girls. "You out on the town tonight?"

Brittany glanced at Bethany, then at Sandra. "Yup. Uncle Logan is buying us an ice cream."

"Then I'd better leave you alone." The last thing Sandra wanted was to come face to face with Logan only half a day after being fired by him.

"Here you are, girls." Logan's deep voice sounded behind her, and Sandra whirled.

Logan looked up and halted, his expression unreadable. "Hello, Sandra," he said, his steady gaze flicking to his nieces and then to her.

"Don't worry," she said crisply. "I haven't had a chance to really corrupt them yet."

Logan said nothing as he handed the cones to the girls. "Why don't you take a walk, Bethany? Brittany?"

The girls giggled and scampered down the beach toward the water.

"I don't think we have anything more to say to each other, Mr. Napier," Sandra said, wrapping her sweater around her. She forced herself to meet his hazel eyes and not to be moved by his casual good looks. A man who wore khaki pants to the beach, whose hair never looked messy, who drove a minivan was exactly the kind of guy her father would love. A conformist. Stifling.

Logan's gaze was steady as he slipped his hands into his back pockets. "I'm sorry that you lost the job—"

"You made me lose the job, Mr. Napier."

"Fair enough. I'm just sorry that it didn't work out."

"It didn't work out because you chose not to let it," Sandra snapped. "You've got your own ideas about who and what I am—"

"I got my ideas from what you told me."

"And based on that you know who I am?"

"Based on what you told me, I'm making a guess." Logan rocked slightly on his heels, still watching her with that unnerving gaze. "I don't think I'm too far off. I have my nieces to think of."

Sandra tried not to get defensive, but she couldn't help it. Everything about him seemed to condemn her out of hand. "Implying that I'm not going to contribute to their well-being."

"Why does this matter so much to you?"

Sandra wasn't sure. It was more than needing the job. Maybe it was because Logan personified the very thing she had been running from, and his judgment stung her pride. Maybe it was because even after spending a couple of days with Brittany and Bethany she was getting attached to the two girls who had lost so much.

Or maybe it was panic at the idea that she had tried to live her life on her own and losing even this small job proved to her the magnitude of her failure.

But Logan didn't need to have one more thing to

judge her by. Didn't need to know precisely how close to the bone she was living right now.

"It doesn't matter," she said quietly, turning away. She took a few steps down the boardwalk, then heard Logan call her.

She didn't want to turn but couldn't stop herself.

"Yes?" she asked, forcing a casual tone to her voice.

"Nothing," he said, lifting his hand as if in surrender. "I'm sorry."

Sandra just nodded and walked on.

"So now what are we going to do?" whispered Brittany as she and Bethany huddled beside each other on the floor of their bedroom. Their lights were out. Below them, they could hear the faint tapping of Uncle Logan's computer keys.

"I thought for sure he would like her," Bethany said wistfully. "And now we have to leave."

Brittany flapped her hand. "So, we'll just have to go ahead with Plan B, I guess."

"What was Plan B?"

Brittany giggled. "Same as Plan A."

"But Plan A was to get Mrs. McKee to leave."

"I was just kidding. But we have to get him and Sandra together again. Just think how cool it would be to have her living with us. I mean Uncle Logan's nice, but…" Brittany shrugged, lifting her hands as if to say, "You know what I mean."

And Bethany did. "He's just not a lot of fun."

"And I'm not going to give up," Brittany insisted. "Not this quick."

Chapter Three

Logan got up from his computer, stretching his arms above his head. It was a nuisance working with this tiny screen when he was used to a much larger monitor at work, but in a pinch it sufficed.

He cocked an ear, listening, but it sounded like the girls had finally drifted off to sleep.

Logan sighed. He had spent most of the day on the phone and still hadn't found a tutor for the girls. No teacher was willing to work for the summer, and no organization had any tutors available.

He saved his work then rubbed his weary eyes. He hadn't gotten as much done as he had hoped between phone calls and trying to concentrate over the girls' chatter. He couldn't catch the concept he aimed for. The Jonserads' vague ideas of light and space were difficult to translate onto a computer screen or paper. It was just a house, but the project was significant. Pass this test and other buildings put up by Jonserad Holdings would be his to design.

Condos, office buildings and gated complexes for senior citizens who didn't want to have to face uninvited children.

A concept Logan could entirely sympathize with.

Logan rubbed the kinks out of his neck and dropped into his recliner. With a sigh he glanced at the clock. Midnight. He knew he should go to bed. *Later*, he thought. *I just want to close my eyes for a few seconds.*

A muffled thump jerked him awake. He sat up, confused and disoriented. The clock struck one.

"Must have fallen asleep," he muttered. Yawning, he got up and stepped into his shoes, not bothering to tie them. He trudged up the stairs to check on his nieces, the tips of the laces ticking on the floor.

Carefully, so as not to wake them, he eased the door open and squinted in the half gloom at the beds.

He frowned at the lumpy outlines of his nieces. They looked odd. A faint breeze riffling through the open window caught his attention. Then he saw the chair. He pulled back the blanket on one of the beds and found rolled-up towels.

Logan stifled an angry sound and spun around. He ran out the door, stepped on a shoelace and promptly hit the hard floor chest first.

Groaning, angry and frustrated, he took the time to tie his laces, then jumped to his feet and took off. His ribs hurt, but his anger fueled him.

Sandra lay back on the prickly grass, pulling the blanket just a little closer around her. The utter quiet was broken by the occasional wail of a coyote in the night, answered in time by another. From horizon to horizon, stars were flung across the velvet black of the sky. Over the crest of the hill behind her lay Elkwater, its few lights faint competition for the glory overhead.

"I see you, Cygna," Sandra whispered, reaching up to trace the cross of the constellation. From there she moved to the brightest stars. "And you, Deneb and Vega and Altair." She let her hand drop and smiled as her eyes drifted over the sky, unable to take in its sheer vastness.

"When I consider the heavens, the works of Thy hands, the moon and the stars which Thou has ordained..." Sandra spoke the words of the Psalms aloud and shivered at how easily they came back to her. She had spent the past few years avoiding the God Who had made all this. Austere, judgmental and demanding.

She had last heard that quote from Brittany and Bethany the night they had sat out here looking at the stars. Sandra was working on astronomy with them, and what better way to study than to actually see it. So, with Florence Napier's blessing, she had taken the girls out late at night to look at the stars.

Bethany and Brittany. Sandra's satisfaction broke as she thought of the girls and, right on the heels of that, of their uncle. His offhand dismissal of her had touched an old wound. One initially opened by her father. She sighed, wondering what it was going to take to finally rid herself of the constant presence of her father's disapproval.

"Hey, Sandra." The sound of young voices drifted to her and she sat up, looking around.

Then she saw the vague outline of two girls running

up the hill. They materialized beside her and dropped down to the grass, panting.

"What are you girls doing here?" she asked, looking past them. She expected to see Logan looming out of the dark. "You're supposed to be in bed."

Brittany shrugged her comment off as she caught her breath. "We need to talk to you. Uncle Logan wants us to go to Calgary with him."

"I know that. He told me. And I don't suppose Uncle Logan knows you're here?" Sandra asked.

In the dim light she saw the girls exchange a quick glance.

Bingo.

"Listen, your uncle already has his own opinion of me, and it isn't what I'd call supportive." Sandra put an arm around each of them. "So if he finds you here, my feeling is he's going to be a little underwhelmed by the whole situation."

The girls giggled.

"Don't worry about Uncle Logan," Brittany said airily, waving a hand as if dismissing her six-foot-two-inch relative.

Sandra didn't think Logan could be gotten rid of that easily. "It's not a good idea to sneak out at night. What if he checks your beds and you're gone? He'd worry."

Brittany and Bethany exchanged another quick glance as if puzzled over this phenomenon. "Our mom and dad never worried when we snuck out at night," Brittany said.

"We didn't even need to sneak."

"Well, I think Uncle Logan is a little different."

Brittany sighed. "He's different, all right. He can barely cook."

"He's learning," Bethany replied in her uncle's defense. "He makes real good pancakes and sausages."

"Sausages aren't hard. Even our mom could make them," Brittany retorted.

"They're hard. You can burn them real quick if you're not careful," Bethany answered, leaning forward to see her sister better. "Uncle Logan doesn't burn them much."

Sandra tried to picture Logan standing in front of a stove, cooking. The thought made her smile, as did Bethany's defense of him.

Brittany turned to Sandra again. "Can't you help us stay? Could you hide us or something?"

Sandra almost laughed at that. "No. I will not hide you, although I will miss you."

"Will we see you before we go?"

"When are you leaving?" Sandra asked.

"In a couple of days."

"I'll probably be on the beach a few times. But I'll be moving on once my car is fixed. I can't stay around here if I don't have a job." Sandra felt a clutch of panic at the thought. A prayer hovered on the periphery of her mind. A cry for help and peace. She shook her head as if to dismiss it. God was a father, after all. Distant, reserved and judging.

She got up and pulled the girls to their feet, giving them each a quick hug. "We'll see each other soon. But now I want you to get back to the house."

They hugged her, their arms clinging. And again

Sandra wondered at their upbringing that they grew so quickly attached to someone they barely knew.

"Go. Now." Sandra gave them a little push and watched as they walked down the hill, going a different way than they had come.

"Bethany, Brittany." Logan's voice, muffled by distance, drifted toward them from another direction.

The girls glanced at Sandra who fluttered an urgent hand at them, then they turned and ran down the shortcut.

"Bethany, Brittany, I know you're up there," Logan called, coming closer.

Sandra winced at the tone of his voice, wrapping her blanket around herself. "He does not sound amused," she whispered, bracing herself as she turned to face him.

Logan's heavy step faltered when he saw who stood on the hill.

"Hey, how's it going?" she asked, adopting a breezy attitude as Logan made it to the top of the hill.

He stood in front of her. Loomed would be a better word, she thought, looking at him in the vague light.

Don't step back. Don't show fear, she reminded herself.

"It's not going good. Where are my nieces?"

Sandra's spine automatically stiffened at his autocratic and accusing tone. "And why do you suppose I would know where they are?"

Logan's hands were planted on his hips, his feet slightly spread, as if he were ready to do battle. Sandra stifled a mixture of fear and admiration at the sight. "Because I'm pretty sure they snuck out to meet you."

It was his tone more than what he said that sparked her temper. That and the remembrance of how he looked down his nose at her the day she had come to teach the girls. The day he had picked her up on the road. "Oh, really?" she asked, her voice hard. "And I suppose I encouraged that?"

He said nothing, and each beat of silence made Sandra fume even as his scrutiny made her feel uncomfortable. His silence and his pose reminded her of intimidating sessions with her father as she struggled to explain herself to him once again. To explain how once again she had failed the great Professor Bachman.

But she was a big girl now. And men like Logan— men like her father—didn't bother her as easily as they used to.

"Your nieces aren't here," she said and turned away from him. The conversation was over.

"I saw their bedroom window open," Logan said, his voice quieter. "I saw a chair under the window."

"Which means what?" she asked, turning to face him. "I'm sure if you were to go down to your house right now you'd find them in bed."

Logan seemed to consider this. "If I talk to them I'll get the truth out of them," he said confidently. "I always do."

"You might. If you push." Sandra wasn't about to either enlighten or lie to him. But some part of her felt sorry for the girls and the confusion of moving from their parents' home to an uncle they had known only briefly. She tried to choose her words, advocating for two girls who, underneath their flighty natures, felt lost and afraid of the future. "I know that if you push children, you can end up pushing them into a lie." She shrugged. "Sometimes you have to choose the battles you want to win."

"You're not defending my nieces, are you?" Logan asked.

In the darkness Sandra couldn't tell from his expression if she had imagined the faint note of humor in his voice.

She lifted one shoulder. "Not really. I just know they really like being here in Cypress Hills. The freedom and the memories, I guess."

"The memories I'll grant them. But they've had enough freedom in their life."

Sandra sighed at the harsh note. "Their parents loved them. Surely that speaks for something."

"It was a strange kind of love, as far as I'm concerned."

Sandra couldn't help but bristle at his comment, memories from her own upbringing clouding her judgment. "What's better? Pushing and forcing your will on them? It's like trying to hold water, Logan. The harder you squeeze, the less control you have."

"You don't understand," he said simply.

"I do, though. I understand far too well."

Logan's eyes seemed to glitter in the dark, and Sandra knew she had overstepped her bounds. But she wasn't going to let him bully her.

"Be careful with them, Logan," she added quietly, sorrow tinging her voice. "They may be spunky, but they're also just young girls."

Logan was quiet a moment. Then without another

word he stepped back, turned and strode down the hill before Sandra could say anything more.

She watched him go, frustrated and confused by him all at the same time. He was bossy, and yet his concern for his nieces touched a part of her that she hadn't paid attention to in a while.

With each step Logan took away from Sandra, his confusion grew. He knew for a fact the girls had been with her. She hadn't said anything, though, and he suspected she was protecting the girls from his wrath.

In spite of his irritation with her, he had to smile. She was concerned about the twins, he gave her that much. He wasn't surprised that Brittany and Bethany were so taken with her. She had a fun sense of humor.

But he had to think of the girls, he reminded himself.

For a moment he yearned for the time when he didn't have the responsibility of two young girls. Young girls were scary enough to take care of outside of the house. Inside, it was chaos and confusion.

He hated chaos and confusion. Had lived with it all his life.

He didn't know what he was going to do if he found the girls in their beds as Sandra had intimated. He couldn't very well accuse them of something he hadn't any true proof of, even if he was the adult in the situation.

Give me wisdom, Lord, he prayed as he had most every day since the girls had dropped into his life. *Give me courage and strength and patience. I don't always know what to do.*

In spite of his confusion, he couldn't help but smile at Sandra's assessment of the situation.

Choose the battles you want to win.

The advice was sound, and he figured it could save him a lot of headaches.

"C'mon, Bethy, it's not that hard. Look, you have to line the numbers up and multiply them." Logan stifled the urge to grab the pencil out of his niece's hand and do the problem himself.

"I can't do it, Uncle Logan. Not when you yell." Bethany frowned at him, chewing on her pencil. "Sandra never got that mad at us."

"Just try it the way I showed you," he said, glancing at Brittany, who quickly looked at her own work. He got up to check it, hoping she at least had understood him.

"No, honey. Look…" He pulled the paper toward him. "You have to make sure that you carry the numbers when there's more than one digit." He showed her and pushed the paper back.

Brittany looked at him, frowning. "What do you mean carry the numbers? Sandra did it better."

"And I suppose she walked on water, too," he muttered.

Logan recognized he wasn't a patient teacher, but he also knew he wasn't too difficult to understand. He knew exactly where his two innocent nieces were leading him. Down the garden path directly to Sandra Bachman's door. Trouble was, after the past few days, he was wondering if maybe he shouldn't just give in.

Yesterday morning, for a few bright and shining moments, he had felt in charge. The girls had come downstairs as if waiting for him to jump on them. Instead he had said nothing, and they seemed confused. They also seemed wary and docile. Logan had felt pretty good.

But the moment of triumph lasted only as long as it took him to get them started on their work.

He was behind on his own work and clinging by his fingernails to the end of his proverbial rope. He still hadn't found a tutor, and each moment he spent with the girls kept him away from his project.

He sighed, looking at the girls as if hoping for one last chance. But they only held his steady gaze, their soft blue eyes unblinking.

So what did he have to lose?

He remembered his condemnation of Sandra and wondered what her reaction to him would be.

Was he being wise? His opinion of her hadn't really changed.

But her comments on how to discipline the girls had lingered. In spite of some of her strange opinions and in spite of her lifestyle, she seemed to have an intuition and basic understanding of how to deal with his nieces. She did have a degree, after all. She couldn't be as flighty as she seemed.

If he hired Sandra it could buy him some time. Time to find a tutor, time to finish his project. It would only be temporary, he reminded himself.

"Okay, let's get this over and done with," he grumbled, walking to the phone. "What's her phone number?"

Brittany and Bethany rattled it off in unison while

Logan punched in the numbers, praying that this was the right decision.

He just didn't have a lot of options left to him.

Sandra knocked on the door of the Napier cabin, smoothed her skirt with her hands, adjusted her shirt and then got mad at herself for doing so. She wasn't going to be nervous, she told herself. Logan was just an uptight person who had changed his mind. Nothing personal.

But when Logan opened the door, she stiffened. She couldn't help feeling defensive, remembering comments he had made the night he had gone looking for his nieces. When he had called her a couple of minutes ago, her first impulse had been to tell him that she was no longer available.

But pride was something only people with money could afford. So she accepted. They laid out the terms and rate of pay, and now she was here, facing a slightly disheveled Logan Napier.

He stood in the doorway, looking at her in that assessing way of his. "Thanks for coming so quickly," he said. "I appreciate it."

A smart answer died as Sandra gave him a closer look.

His dark hair looked like he had been running his fingers through it, and today he wore jeans and a T-shirt. Not quite as put together as when she had first met him. In fact, he looked worn out. In spite of their moments of antagonism, Sandra felt a gentle softening toward him.

"The girls are in the kitchen, trying to figure out how to cross multiply," he added with a heavy sigh.

Sandra frowned. "They know how to do that."

"I thought so, too." Logan smiled a mirthless smile. "But it seems to have slipped their minds since you stopped working with them. Amazing coincidence."

"Must be the air," she said with a careful lift of her eyebrows, acknowledging his attempt at reconciliation.

"Must be." Logan stepped back, allowing her to enter. "Just come with me a moment. We need to go over a few things before you start."

Sandra swallowed, toying with the idea of asking him for an advance. As she followed him through the cabin, she decided against it. She didn't need to reinforce his idea that she was a freeloader. She'd have to get along as best she could until she'd worked for at least a week, she thought, following him into his office.

"I need to emphasize that this job is only temporary," he said with a piercing look. "You shouldn't have too much trouble with that."

"Just like every other job I've held," Sandra couldn't help but add.

Logan didn't even blink. He looked her straight in the eye. "Then this should work out just fine for you."

Sandra felt a shiver of animosity. But she knew she couldn't indulge in her usual antics. Like it or not, Logan was her boss, and her situation here was tenuous.

She swallowed her pride and nodded. "I better get to it, then," she said quietly.

"I'm going to be working in the bedroom down here. If you need anything." He looked at the papers he was organizing on his drafting table.

Feeling dismissed, Sandra bit her lip and walked out of the room, angry that she had ever seen him as helpless. About as helpless as a grizzly, she thought.

Then she walked into the kitchen to be greeted with shouts of happiness and hugs from the girls. It helped to negate some of her anger at Logan. But not totally dissipate it.

Logan pulled out another sheet of paper, his frustration growing. He had an idea in his head of how he wanted the Jonserad house to look. He could close his eyes and just about picture it, but always when he put pencil to paper, the thoughts wouldn't translate.

He stretched his neck and glanced out the window. He saw a family walking down the road. Mom and Dad were carrying a picnic hamper between them, beach towels slung over their shoulders. Two young boys ran ahead, carrying inflatable beach toys. Off for a day of sun and water, he thought with a slight pang of jealousy.

But he had work to do, and so did the girls. They had spent enough of their childhood running around carefree. They really needed to work.

And so did he, if he wanted the project, he reminded himself.

As he picked up another pencil, he heard the sound of muffled laughter. Then Sandra's laugh pealed out, stifled to a giggle. What humor could they possibly find in doing math?

It sounded as though they had moved from the kitchen to the main room. What were they doing there? He got up to check when things got very quiet.

The girls were sprawled on the living room floor. Brittany was chewing on a pencil while she frowned at a problem she worked on, and Sandra lay on the floor between them, quietly explaining something to Bethany. Her hair hung like a shimmering curtain over her shoulder. With an impatient gesture she pushed it back, exposing the fine line of her jaw, her smiling mouth.

Logan caught himself staring at her. Attractive or no, he wasn't too sure about her teaching arrangements. "Shouldn't you girls be sitting at a table?" Logan asked.

"I suggested that we move to a place that's a little more comfortable," Sandra said, sitting up.

Logan frowned at her quick reply. "I can't see that you'll get much done laying all over the floor."

Bethany's and Brittany's heads shot up, and Sandra motioned to the girls to go back to their work as she got up.

"Can I talk to you a moment, Mr. Napier?" she asked.

"Sure."

Sandra walked past Logan to his office. Momentarily taken aback, he couldn't help but follow.

Once inside the room, Sandra turned to face him. "I understand your concern about the girls and I appreciate that. But I think I need to establish something right from the beginning. This job may be temporary." She paused, glancing at him through narrowed eyes. "But I'm their teacher and I'll decide on the teaching methods."

Logan scowled, uncomfortable with how quickly she

took charge. "I guess I need to make something clear, too, Miss Bachman. I'm their guardian and I'm the one who hired you," he countered.

Sandra crossed her arms as if ready to face him down. "That's correct. But you came to me, I didn't come to you. You recognized that I have abilities and training, and in order for me to do my job, I need you to just let me do it."

"And if I don't like your methods?"

"Then I guess you'll be teaching them on your own." Her deep brown eyes held his. She tipped her head ever so slightly. "Just like you were doing when you called me."

Logan swallowed, fighting down the urge to tell this snippy woman that she could leave. He'd been in charge of his nieces for a year and a half without any outside help, thank you very much. He didn't appreciate being told to back off and let someone else take over.

However, as she had so diplomatically pointed out, teaching the girls on his own wasn't working, and he didn't have any alternative available to him.

He couldn't give up so easily. Not with her. "That sounds like a threat, Sandra Bachman."

She shook her head, smiling lightly. "No threat, Logan Napier. Just setting out boundaries."

Logan had to regain some ground. He forced himself to smile. "Just so you realize, these girls need to go back to formal schooling in September. They won't be able to lay on the floor in their classroom."

Sandra's smile stiffened. "Formal school." She laughed lightly. "It never ceases to amaze me that curiosity and adventure manage to survive formal education.''

Logan wondered if he imagined the caustic note in her voice. ''That's an interesting comment, coming from you,'' he said, testing her. ''Formal education gave you a degree, even though you don't seem to be doing much with it.''

Sandra straightened, her eyes narrowed, and Logan knew he had stepped over an invisible boundary. ''I'm teaching your nieces with it, Mr. Napier,'' she said. ''And I had better get back to it.'' She tossed him a look that clearly told him the subject was closed, and with a swish of her skirt, she left.

Logan felt momentarily taken aback at her abrupt exit. He hoped he had made his point with her, though he wasn't sure how he came out of that little skirmish. Sandra was a puzzle, that much he knew.

And a puzzle she would stay, he thought. As long as she was teaching his girls, he would keep his eye on her, but her private life would remain private as far as he was concerned.

He went to his computer and dropped into the chair. As he struggled with a plan that was finally coming together, he couldn't help but pause once in a while, listening to the husky tones of Sandra's voice as she patiently explained the vagaries of mathematics.

Later he heard Sandra telling the girls what she wanted them to work on that evening. He got up and wandered into the living room, ostensibly to establish his so-called parental involvement.

''Work on the rest of chapter four in your math

books," she said, writing on a piece of paper. "And I want you to go over some of the history material."

"But history is so boring," Brittany said with a pout. "Especially this stuff."

"History is just a story that you have to discover," Sandra said.

Logan could see from Brittany's expression that she wasn't convinced.

"Hey, a lot of the history you are studying happened right here." Sandra chucked Brittany lightly under the chin. "In Cypress Hills."

"Really?" Brittany didn't sound like she believed Sandra.

"Fort Walsh was an important place in the late eighteen hundreds. And it's part of Cypress Hills Park," Sandra explained. "On the Saskatchewan side."

"Could we go there?"

"That would be a good idea, but I have no way of bringing you there." Sandra lifted her hands as if in surrender. "Sorry."

The girls turned as one to Uncle Logan. He recognized the gleam in their eyes and knew what was coming.

"You could give us the van, Uncle Logan," Brittany said with an ingenuous smile.

Logan shook his head. "Now why did I know you were going to say that?"

Brittany shrugged, a delicate movement that would one day drive some young boy crazy. "I don't know."

He wasn't going to look at Sandra but couldn't stop himself. She held his gaze, her own slightly mocking.

"I don't have time to bring you," he said.

"Uncle Logan," Brittany said. "You have to."

"I think your uncle Logan is too busy working to come with us, Brittany," Sandra said with a lift of her chin.

Logan couldn't help but pick up the challenging note in her voice.

"Not all of us have the luxury of doing what we want, Miss Bachman."

"Oh, yes, we do. It's all in what we choose to give up to do what we want. You've chosen to sit inside and work instead of enjoying the wonderful outdoors."

"I've chosen to try to make a living," he said with a short laugh.

Sandra held his gaze for a split second, then looked away, a faint grin teasing her mouth. "If that's what you want to call it."

Logan was about to defend himself, to explain how necessary this project was, when a faint niggling doubt wormed its way into his subconscious. He remembered seeing the family going to the beach this morning. He thought of the project he wasn't having much luck putting together. Maybe some time off with the girls would be good for him.

And, he reasoned, he could keep an eye on Sandra Bachman. After all, the girls were his responsibility, and she had only been teaching them for a short time.

Brittany sensed his hesitation and jumped on it. "So, are you going to come with us, Uncle Logan?"

"Please, Uncle Logan?" Bethany added her entreaty.

He looked at the two girls and wondered if there was

ever going to come a time that he wouldn't give in to them.

"I could do that," he said, careful to make it look as if his capitulation came at a price. "If Ms. Bachman doesn't mind," he added as a concession to Sandra.

"Seeing as how Ms. Bachman doesn't own a set of working wheels, Ms. Bachman doesn't mind at all," Sandra said, finally looking up from the paper she held. "As long as Mr. Napier is willing to work with me."

Logan recognized the challenge and rose to it. "I believe in being diplomatic, Ms. Bachman."

She smiled. "Ah, yes. Diplomacy. The art of letting people have your own way."

Logan couldn't help the smile that tugged on his mouth at her snappy answer and decided to let it go. He sensed that he would be the loser in a verbal battle with Sandra.

"So set a time and we'll be ready to leave," he said.

"First thing tomorrow morning," Sandra replied. "I'd like to go before it gets too hot."

"We'll be ready."

As the innocuous words were tossed back and forth, Logan stifled the faint dart of pleasure at the idea of spending time with Sandra. He was only coming along to supervise. That was all.

Chapter Four

"So how did you like a taste of Whoop Up Country?" Sandra asked as they left the stockaded fort known as Farwell's Trading Post.

"Hot," Bethany said, fanning herself with a brochure.

"Can you imagine what it was like in those days when no one had air-conditioning?" Sandra asked with a laugh. She lifted her hair from her damp neck, wishing she had worn it up.

"You girls would have roasted in those long dresses they had to wear in those days," Logan added.

The girls groaned in sympathy.

"Men didn't have it a whole lot better," Sandra added, glancing at Logan's short-sleeved shirt. "You look a lot cooler than Farwell, owner of the trading post. Or how about those poor Mounties in their red serge. Hot, hot, hot."

Heat waves shimmered from the ground, attesting to

how warm it really was. The short grass crunched under their feet as they walked toward the tour bus.

"I can't imagine how the grass even grows here, it's so warm." Brittany poked the ground with her toe.

"This grass is very high in protein," Sandra explained. "The buffalo survived quite nicely on it. That's how Fort Benton, in Montana, got started. It was a fur and buffalo robe trading post stuck in the middle of buffalo country. From Fort Benton, traders for both furs and whiskey ended up taking the Whoop Up Trail into Canada where there was nothing but trouble. No law, no rules. People did what they wanted."

"So how did that stop?" Bethany asked.

Sandra paused, looking at the hills. So peaceful, it was hard to believe that at one time the fear-filled cries of Lakota Indians rang through these hills. As she retold the story of the Cypress Hills Massacre, she tried to inject a feeling of humanity—putting a human face to the story—into what was often mere facts and history. She could feel the girls looking first at her, then at the hills. Even Logan listened intently as she spoke.

The silence that followed her story told her she had done her job.

"After the massacre the Canadian government sent the Northwest Mounted Police, later known as the Royal Canadian Mounted Police, to this area. They started out from Manitoba and ended up in Fort Benton to replenish their supplies and get some information on the massacre. When they came to the place Fort Macleod is now, the whiskey traders had taken off. Knew the Mounties were coming." Sandra winked at Brittany, relieving the heavy atmosphere her sad story had created. "Knew the Mounties always get their man."

She answered a few more questions the girls had, trying each time to work in some pertinent information. She knew that history told was one thing but history experienced meant much more.

She also knew that history, even when told in an entertaining manner, was only interesting for a short period of time.

"I guess we should head back to the main fort now," she said, noticing the shuttle bus pulling into the parking lot.

Bethany and Brittany hurried toward it.

"Hey, girls. Slow down," Logan called, but the girls didn't hear. Or pretended not to.

"Relax, Uncle Logan," Sandra said with a grin at how protective he was. "They're not going anywhere we aren't."

"Maybe, but it's still too hot to run."

Sandra frowned. "My goodness, Logan, they won't melt. From what they told me, they've been in warmer climates than this."

Logan's gaze sliced sideways, then back. "They told you about their parents?"

"Just a little."

She waited to hear something, anything, more, but he didn't offer any information. Merely stepped aside so Sandra could get on the bus.

Without looking at Logan, Sandra walked to an empty seat directly behind the girls and sat down. To her surprise, Logan sat beside her.

Brittany and Bethany glanced back and immediately moved to the front, but Logan stayed where he was.

She wanted to ask him more about the girls' parents but didn't think that he would be very forthcoming.

But with each lurch of the bus, Sandra grew more self-conscious, more aware of him sitting silently beside her. He said nothing, did nothing, but Sandra felt every time his elbow brushed hers, each time a hole in the road threw her against him.

She pulled herself closer to the side of the bus and away from him, turning to stare out the window.

The bus stopped, and the girls were the first ones out. By the time Logan and Sandra got out, the girls were waiting for them, full of good cheer. "Can we have some ice cream, Uncle Logan?" Bethany asked, tipping her head coyly. "Pretty please?"

Logan was already digging in his pocket. He pulled out a bill. He glanced sidelong at Sandra, his dark brows pulled together in a light frown. "These girls have an insatiable appetite for ice cream. Do you want one?"

Sandra shook her head. "No, thanks."

"I'll wait out here for you then," Logan said, handing the bill to the girls. "And I expect to see the change."

Brittany and Bethany flashed him demure smiles, shared a grin and ran into the building.

Without looking at Logan, Sandra turned and walked up the hill overlooking the valley, then sat down, determined to put some space between her and Logan.

But to her surprise, Logan followed her and sat beside her. She pulled her knees up, wrapping her arms around them. She resented the awkwardness he created in her, and she tried not to let it show.

The best defense is offense, she thought.

"So, you aren't chafing to get back to your work," she said, her heightened reaction to him giving her voice an unexpected bite.

Logan leaned back, resting his weight on his elbows. He looked over the valley below them. He seemed surprisingly at ease.

"I can do this," he said, tucking his chin on his chest. "Even though I do need to get back to work."

"Ah, yes. Uncle Logan the upwardly mobile man." Sandra couldn't stop the little gibe. It seemed better to put him on the defensive rather than to look at him and notice the faint wave to his hair, how it curled over his ears.

The way his sudden smile eased the harsh line of his features.

"Do you ever run out of smart remarks?" he asked.

"I think life is too serious to be taken seriously," she replied.

Logan let out a short laugh. But he didn't answer her question.

Note to self, she thought, biting her lip. *No more smart comments. At least not to Logan Napier.*

She wasn't usually this flip. Usually she could carry on a normal, intelligent conversation, but Logan's calm self-possession touched a nerve.

At any rate, she had better learn to put a curb on her tongue if she wanted to stay in Logan's good graces and keep this job.

She looked over the sweep of the valley. The hills

here were softened, smoothed by the wind that swept across the open plains of Montana and Saskatchewan and sifted around this oasis in the prairie. She sighed lightly, waiting for the utter peace of the place to slowly soothe the tension she felt sitting beside Logan. But try as she might, she couldn't ignore his strong presence.

And he seemed content to just sit, saying nothing.

Once again, his silence unnerved her. In spite of her resolution, she sought to find something, anything to ease the discomfort he created.

"So how long have the girls been living with you?" she asked, resting her chin on her knees.

Logan plucked a blade of grass, twirling it between his fingers. "About a year and a half."

"Did they come right after their parents died?"

Logan nodded, still looking away.

"That must have been difficult," she said quietly.

"It was. At first. I think kids grieve differently than adults do. They dive in deep and hard, but they come out of it quicker. Their sadness is different...." Logan stopped, twirling the grass faster.

"Different than what?" Sandra prompted.

He looked at her then. "Different than adults, I was going to say."

"Their mother was your sister, wasn't she?" Sandra asked, holding his steady gaze, wondering at their relationship.

"She was my only sibling. Flighty. Strange. But still my sister."

For a moment Sandra envied him even that. "How did you get along?"

Logan pushed himself to a sitting position. "Pretty good. When I was younger we depended heavily on each other. We switched schools so many times the only person we knew in school was each other."

"Your parents traveled that much?"

Logan laughed, but it held no humor. "Endlessly. Every few months we would pack up and be gone again. My father died a while ago, but my mother still travels a lot."

Sandra sighed, thinking of her upbringing. "Sounds kind of neat."

"I'm sure to you it would," Logan said dryly. He got up, held her gaze a moment, then looked down the hill.

"Here come the girls," he said, brushing off his pants.

And once again Sandra felt as if she had been weighed and found wanting.

And once again it bothered her.

Chapter Five

Logan watched as the girls dawdled up the hill toward them. He was about to call to them when they suddenly turned and ran to the visitors' center. He started off after them.

"What are they doing?" he heard Sandra ask as she caught up to him.

Logan knew all too well what they were up to and decided it would be better if everything was out in the open.

"My dear nieces can't stand the idea that I don't currently have a girlfriend," he said dryly, glancing at her. "They're avoiding us because they have grand visions of playing matchmaker."

Sandra laughed.

To his chagrin, Logan felt deflated at her reaction. "What can I say," he said, wishing he had her quick, glib tongue. "They're young."

"Some day they'll grow up, Logan Napier."

Logan sighed. "I pray for it daily."

"Do you?"

He turned, looking fully at her. "Yes. I do."

Sandra's gaze flicked sideways then back. "I remember you said that you go to church."

"Why does that always come out with a faint note of mockery?" he asked as he reached the sidewalk at the bottom of the hill.

"Like I told you before, I'm not a church person."

"Why not?" He stopped, turning to face her. He wanted to know more about this part of her life. After all, she was teaching his nieces.

"It's full of hypocrites," she said airily.

"That's the oldest excuse in the book."

Sandra's dark brown eyes met his, unable to conceal the sparkle that lit at his challenge. "What book?"

"Pardon me?" Logan asked.

"What book is that the oldest excuse in? Is there a book somewhere full of excuses? And if there is, how do you know it's the oldest one? What if it's the newest?" Sandra threw out the questions one after the other, a smile curving her lips.

In spite of his exasperation with her, Logan laughed. "I'm not even going to start a battle of words with you," he said. "But I will challenge your hypocrite comment. You have to admit that using that excuse is pretty lame. There are hypocrites in every organization. Where there are people, there are failings."

Sandra cocked her head as if thinking. "Okay. I'll concede that point. Begrudgingly," she added, pointing a finger at him. "Don't want to let you off too easy."

"So why don't you go to church?" Logan asked.

"I believe in God, Logan. Just in case that's what

you're really wondering. I just don't believe that church fills any need of mine. I prefer to worship God in nature.''

Logan felt a stab of disappointment. He didn't know what he had hoped for, but her answer brushed away some faint hope he had harbored. A hope that didn't really have anything to do with his nieces' well-being. ''But nature doesn't tell you of the need for redemption, Sandra,'' he replied quietly.

Sandra's answer was a dismissive shrug.

Right then the girls came out of the building, pretending surprise to see Logan and Sandra.

''Let's look at the rest of the site,'' Sandra said, forestalling any recriminations or feeble explanations.

The girls followed Sandra while Logan lagged behind, listening as she explained the history of Fort Walsh.

''Later, in the nineteen forties, the RCMP purchased this site and set up Remount Ranch to breed and raise their horses. They also raised and trained the horses for the Musical Ride here.''

''I've heard of the Musical Ride,'' Logan said. ''But what exactly is it?''

''A riding display developed from traditional cavalry drills. It's very impressive. I believe 32 horses and riders are involved.''

''We saw that,'' Bethany offered. ''In Texas. At a rodeo. It was awesome. Those black horses. And the riders in those neat red coats.''

Logan wasn't surprised at that. Linda and her husband traveled enough different places, they were bound to have crossed paths at one time or another with the RCMP's Musical Ride.

The rest of the tour went fast. To her credit, Sandra could tell when the girls' interest waned, and would quickly move on to the next place. They walked through barracks and living quarters, then took a picture by the flagpole in the center of the fort. Logan operated the camera, smiling as Bethany and Brittany crowded right up beside Sandra.

He looked through the lens and adjusted the zoom lens, bringing the little group in closer. Sandra looked up, smiling, and Logan couldn't suppress the tug of attraction. Sandra's open smile suffused her entire being and made him want to laugh along with her.

He snapped the picture, recognizing Sandra's beauty and at the same time realizing that any man would be attracted to her. And that was all he felt, he reminded himself. Just a basic recognition of her appeal. He didn't have the time or the inclination to take anything further from there. Not with someone like Sandra.

The drive back was quiet. Both girls slept in the back seat, which meant, Logan thought with a sigh, that they would be awake and giddy for most of the evening. Looked like he wasn't going to get much done tonight.

Sandra didn't say much. Just looked ahead, her expression serious. Logan couldn't help but glance at her once in a while, wondering what she was thinking.

Logan wondered if his comment about church had made the usually loquacious Sandra Bachman retreat into silence. He doubted it. Someone as self-possessed as Sandra wasn't the kind of person to be intimidated by someone else's opinion.

But her silence made him feel uncomfortable. As they neared Elkwater, she picked up her knapsack, fiddling with the zippers and buckles.

"Just drop me off at the gas station," she said as he made the long turn into the town.

"Tell me where you live and I'll drop you off," Logan said.

"No. Please. I want to go for a walk. Maybe even a swim," she said with a forced laugh, pushing her hair from her face.

Logan slowed and stopped at the gas station as she had requested. "Are you sure you don't want me to bring you to your house?" he asked once again, feeling most unchivalrous.

"No. Thanks. I really want to walk." She glanced at the girls, who were still sleeping, their cheeks flushed with the heat and the sun. "Say goodbye to the girls. Tell them I'll see them on Monday."

Logan nodded, bending over as Sandra got out of the van. She paused, holding on to the door, and glanced at him. "Thanks for driving us to the fort," she said. "I had a good time."

"You're welcome. I learned a lot today," he said with a quick grin. "Thanks for that."

"Nice to be able to put my expensive education to some use," she returned. "Have a good evening." She turned and walked away, her skirt swaying.

Logan knew he should drive away. Knew he shouldn't be watching Sandra, shouldn't be allowing his basic attraction to her good looks take over his common sense.

But he had enjoyed the day with her, and even

though part of him disapproved, he had to laugh at her quick tongue, her pert responses. Once again he smiled at some of the things she had said.

Then he glanced at the girls, dismayed to see Brittany awake and looking at him with frank interest.

"What are we waiting for, Uncle Logan?" she asked, her voice radiating innocence.

"Traffic," he replied, deadpan. Then, without a second glance, he drove to their house.

Sandra pulled out her last sheet of ruby glass, setting it carefully on the light table. With a felt pen she marked the places she would cut, working with the striations and the patterns inherent in the glass.

She smiled as she envisioned how the completed lamp would look, how the light would play through it.

So far she had enough glass for one lamp and a few pieces left over for a second. She had hoped to pick up her glass shipment, still sitting in a warehouse in Medicine Hat. But she would have to wait until she got her first tutoring paycheck. It surprised her that Logan was willing to pay her more than Florence had offered. Of course, he could probably afford it, she reasoned.

She didn't know how long the job would last, but so far she calculated that if she worked one more day, she would have enough money to pay for the glass. Three more days would pay for her car, and four more days would earn a few more groceries that would last until the lamps were finished.

A small thrill of excitement fluttered through her at the thought of completing the lamp and what the job represented. Money earned on her own and maybe, perhaps, the beginning of a new career.

For now, it looked as if she would be able to prove her father wrong, after all. Her life was finally coming to a place of her own choosing.

She pulled out the patterns for the petals of the flowers, and as she laid them on the glass, she happened to look out the window.

If she angled her head slightly, she could see the front door of the church in Elkwater. She had never attended. As she had told Logan, her preferred place of worship was up on a hill, away from other people. Alone and away from the harsh expectations she'd grown up with.

But today she caught herself looking at the church more than once as she worked. Wondered what kind of people went. Wondered if they sang any of the traditional songs that were sung in her church.

She hadn't been to church since she left home five years ago. She had thrown off the stifling expectations of her father, and church attendance was one of them.

She'd been in Elkwater for four months, and only in the last two had she started eyeing the church.

And that was mostly because Cora, her good friend and fellow traveler, had left again.

If anyone could talk her out of going, Cora could, Sandra thought, looking at the glass she was preparing to cut. She and Cora had been through a lot together. California, Minnesota and at the end, Hornby Island and Henri Desault.

Sandra shivered. Henri was too vivid a memory still. She wouldn't be in the financial pickle she was in if it wasn't for Henri and his smooth talking. A consummate salesman, she thought, curling her lip in disgust. She set the pattern on the glass, tracing it with quick, decisive strokes as if trying to eradicate the memory.

She had spent time with Henri. Had dated him and thought she'd found someone who cared about her. Who accepted her without expectations. Then one day she let him see the stained glass work she did in her spare time. Time she'd eked away from the mindless day jobs she needed to pay for her supplies. She'd planned on selling her work when she had enough inventory built up. The money was going to finance her working full time on her own.

Henri knew a place to sell her stuff and promised her more money than she could get peddling at craft fairs and local markets.

She had fallen for his charm, his smooth talk, and in no time, seven of her best pieces of work had been taken and sold. She had trusted him to return. Trusted him to give her the money.

She hadn't seen a penny from Henri. Nor had she seen Henri again.

At that low point in her life, Cora came up with the brain wave of moving to Alberta.

Sandra had fought the move. Anywhere in Alberta was too close to Calgary and home. But the thought of staying alone was even more depressing.

So she gamely packed up her little car with the few things she and Cora owned. They worked their way through the Fraser Valley, then across Alberta to Medicine Hat. There they found an ad for a small furnished house for rent in the town of Elkwater. It had an extra room for Sandra to set up a studio of sorts. Sandra sold a few pieces, and through that got the order for the lamps.

Now Cora was gone, with a promise that as soon as she returned, they would head south to California. But the longer Cora stayed away, the less sure Sandra was of leaving. In fact, it seemed that in the past six months, Sandra's dissatisfaction with her life had grown.

She missed belonging somewhere. And whether she wanted to admit it or not, she missed belonging to someone.

She glanced out the window. A movement at the church made Sandra pay closer attention. The doors opened and a few people walked out.

She wasn't going to watch, she thought.

But she couldn't stop herself from looking. Bethany and Brittany bounced out of the church, their facial expressions exaggerated as they chatted with each other. Sandra smiled and kept looking, wondering.

And there he was. Behind them, hands in the pockets of his eternal khaki pants, came their uncle Logan.

He was smiling, looking relaxed, at peace.

Sandra felt a mixture of envy and a lift of pleasure as she watched him. He was good-looking, she had to concede. He had the potential to be a lot of fun, if only he'd drop the fussy, protective-uncle shtick he insisted on maintaining.

He paused, looking back to say something to a young woman who caught up to him. She wore a beige shift. Neat. Elegant. Uptight, Sandra thought a bit cattily.

Logan's smile grew as he spoke to the woman. He lifted his hand and touched her shoulder lightly. It was almost avuncular, but for the first time in many years, Sandra felt a distinct dig of jealousy at the gesture. Around Sandra, Logan was either uptight, thinking she might lead his nieces astray, or he was scowling, thinking she might lead his nieces astray.

He was worse than some of the parents she had met while student teaching.

Yet she couldn't keep her eyes off him as he talked to the woman.

She wondered who she was. Friend? Girlfriend who had come up for a visit?

Sandra took a deep breath, as if cleansing away the coil of strange emotions, and concentrated on tracing exactly twelve petals on the glass. She made a mistake and rubbed it out with a tissue then glanced out the window again.

But Logan, the woman and the girls were gone.

She felt momentarily bereft. Left out. She didn't belong to that little group. She was here in her rented house. They were out there, heading to Logan's spacious cabin.

This was enough, she told herself.

She capped her pen, dropped it on her worktable and headed to the beach, open spaces and other people.

"I'd love to go for a walk." As Karen stood, she addressed the girls, who were laying on the floor, playing a board game. "Are you coming, Brittany and Bethany?"

Logan saw them exchange a quick look, and it

wasn't kind. He knew they would say no. They had never really liked Karen.

"We'd love to," Brittany said, getting up. "Wouldn't we Bethany?"

Bethany nodded, smiling at her uncle, who looked at both his nieces, his eyes narrowed. Why the sudden change of heart?

"We'll clean the game up after, Uncle Logan," Brittany said, smiling at him.

They were up to something. He knew it. He angled his body away from Karen. He shot them both a warning look that he knew Karen wouldn't see.

They quickly glanced down, and he knew the message was sent and understood. Behave.

He turned to Karen with a forced smile. "Shall we go?"

The afternoon sun warmed Logan's shoulders as they walked in silence to the lake.

Logan was still trying to absorb the shock he had felt when Karen showed up unexpectedly on his doorstep this morning.

She had been passing through, she had said. Stayed overnight in Medicine Hat. Logan's partner told her where he was. She thought, since she was in the neighborhood, maybe she would stop in and see how Logan and the girls were doing.

Brittany and Bethany stayed close by as they walked, as if unwilling to give Karen and Logan the space they always gave him and Sandra.

"Your partner, Ian, tells me that you've got an important project due," Karen said, breaking the silence.

Logan nodded. "I'm submitting it on spec. A few

other architects are submitting plans, as well. If the client likes what I've done, we have a good chance at more work.'' He bit his lip, thinking of the project that just wouldn't obey. He'd never had this hard a time coming up with ideas. Nor had so much been riding on one project, he reminded himself.

''I heard it was the Jonserads that you might be doing this work for.'' Karen angled him a questioning glance. ''They're a pretty big company. Family business.''

Logan nodded. He didn't need the reminder.

''My parents know the Jonserads,'' she added coyly. ''If you want, I could put in a good word for you.''

Logan stiffened at the suggestion. All his life he had worked for everything he had. Nothing had come easily. He had managed without anyone's help, and he was proud of that.

''Thanks for that, Karen. But I would just as soon earn the job based on my own merit.'' He smiled at her to ease the harshness of his words. But he could tell from the suddenly brittle smile that she was hurt.

''The girls seem to be settling down,'' Karen said with forced brightness as she wrapped her sweater around herself.

Thankfully Brittany and Bethany had gone a little ahead, talking and laughing.

''It's taken a bit of doing, but it's coming along.'' Logan slipped his hands in his pockets, squinting against the glare of the sun off the lake. He wondered again why Karen had come.

They arrived at the boardwalk that led partway

around the lake. Karen's steps slowed. She was letting the girls get even farther ahead.

"I know my coming here is a surprise," she said quietly, looking straight ahead. "I'm sure you thought, after I broke up with you, that you'd never see me again."

Logan said nothing, letting her do all the talking. Their break had caused him a measure of pain, but in retrospect, he realized that his pride had hurt more than his feelings.

"This is a little awkward for me." She sighed and stopped, turning to face him, lifting her exquisite face to his. Her short blond hair framed her features perfectly, emphasizing her delicate cheekbones, the fine line of her chin. Logan recognized her beauty almost as an afterthought. Which surprised him, considering that at one time he'd been attracted to her.

"I realized how much I missed you, Logan," she continued, her soft green eyes holding his. "When the girls came, I made a rash decision. I see that now."

"It was a while ago, Karen," he gently reminded her. Eighteen months, to be precise, he thought.

"I know. That's what makes this so awkward." She smiled at him, tentatively reaching out to him. "I tried to date other guys. I thought I could forget you." She shrugged her dainty shoulders, wrapped by her finely knit cardigan. "I couldn't."

Logan nodded, wondering how to extricate himself from this situation. Karen might have been yearning to try again, but he had no inclination to renew the relationship. Not with his work and his nieces occupying most of his time.

Where were those girls when he needed them?

As if on cue, he heard Brittany call, "Uncle Logan, look who we found."

He glanced up with a grin of relief that faded when he saw their reluctant escort.

Sandra Bachman.

Brittany had one of her hands, Bethany the other, and they were pulling her along the boardwalk.

The girls stopped in front of Karen and Logan, looking at Sandra like they had just snagged a prize.

"She was coming this way already," Bethany said, bestowing an angelic smile on Logan.

"I was just heading home, actually," Sandra said. The soft breeze coming off the lake teased her loose hair, made her long flowing skirt sway. She looked soft, deceptively gentle. Logan couldn't look away.

Her dark eyes flicked over Karen, then to Logan, one eyebrow quirking when she noticed his regard.

Covering up, Logan turned to Karen. "I should introduce you to the girls' tutor, Sandra Bachman. Sandra, this is…Karen."

Karen seemed to catch his momentary hesitation over her official title, but recovered and put on a polite smile, extending her hand to Sandra.

"Nice to meet you," Karen said smoothly.

Sandra shook her hand, her gaze assessing. "Likewise," she said, one corner of her mouth curling into a smile.

Logan braced himself for one of Sandra's comments, but she said nothing more.

"So the girls must keep you quite busy," Karen said.

Sandra glanced at each of the girls. "They're a challenge that I try to rise to every day. But I think we're making some progress."

Karen murmured a vague response, then looked at Logan, as if expecting him to end this conversation.

But Logan knew what faced him if he was alone with Karen again. He didn't feel inclined to reopen the topic of Karen and her feelings on their relationship.

"Out for some exercise?" he asked Sandra, slipping his hands in his pockets, projecting the image of someone with nothing better to do than chat up his nieces' tutor.

"No, just a walk," Sandra replied with a sparkle in her eye. "I get enough exercise just pushing my luck."

Logan couldn't help his answering grin. "And here I thought you were the kind of person who would spend hours in aerobic classes."

Sandra waved that comment away. "I'd sooner spend my money on chocolate fudge sundaes than pay someone to put me through pain."

"If you've experienced pain while doing aerobics, that could be the fault of your instructor," Karen informed her.

Logan glanced sidelong at Karen, feeling a faint flush of shame at how completely he had ignored her.

"Could be," Sandra agreed, her grin fading as she looked at Karen. "Or it could be that I just wasn't doing things right." Sandra took an abrupt step back, and Logan recognized the first movement toward departure. The quick glance at her watch was the second.

He didn't want her to go.

"It's been nice meeting you, Karen," she said, formal. Polite.

Karen smiled in return.

But the girls weren't happy. "We just got here. You can't go now, Sandra," Brittany wailed.

Sandra laid a hand on each of their shoulders, still grinning. "I have two legs, and in spite of not taking aerobics, I can walk quite well. No 'can't' about it."

"Then you shouldn't go," Bethany corrected, grabbing Sandra's hand.

"And shouldn't is a moral imperative, Bethany." Sandra tapped Bethany's nose. "I'm on my day off, so I'm not under any obligation to follow it."

Logan couldn't help but smile at the word games Sandra so easily indulged in. But it was better for all concerned, himself included, if they kept their relationship arm's-length.

"Let's go, Bethy, Brit," Logan said, hastening the separation. "We shouldn't waste Sandra's time."

In spite of his reflections, he couldn't help another glance in her direction and was disconcerted to see her looking at him, as well, her expression serious.

Then, with a quick wave and a toss of her head, Sandra was striding down the boardwalk toward the beach, her hair and skirt swinging in time with her steps.

"So, that's the new tutor," Karen said, a prim note in her voice. "She seems very…vivacious."

Logan's only acknowledgment of Karen's statement was a curt nod. As he glanced at Karen, he couldn't help comparing the two women. Sandra's dark eyes, dark hair and wide smile. Karen's light hair, clear eyes and composed manner.

Shaking his head, he pushed the thoughts aside. Karen had come to church. Sandra hadn't. That should be comparison enough for him.

Karen stayed until late afternoon. She coerced the girls into a board game, talked with Logan about friends they had in common.

But when she drove away and he came into the cabin, he felt worn out and was thankful to be alone again.

"You're not going back to her, are you?" Brittany asked as soon as he stepped into the house. She lay on the couch, Bethany on the recliner. Both had their eyes fixed on their uncle.

Logan looked at his more outspoken niece, weighing his words. "That's not for you to say, Brittany," he replied firmly, recognizing the need to set personal boundaries. "Karen is a good person, and at one time we had a strong relationship."

"Why did she come back?"

"She just came for a visit." Logan wasn't going to delve into the real reason. Given the girls' antagonism toward his former girlfriend and their not so subtle cheerleading for Sandra, he figured the less they knew, the better.

Brittany gave her uncle a knowing look. "I bet she wants you back."

Logan was taken aback at Brittany's perceptiveness.

"I've seen the way she looks at you," Brittany said smugly. "What do you think, Bethany?"

Bethany gave a hesitant shrug. "I don't know."

Brittany snorted. "Of course, you don't know. She liked *you*." Brittany looked at her uncle. "I think she wants you back."

"And I think you've said enough, Brittany," Logan chided, walking past her to the kitchen. "Seeing as how you're so full of advice, you can help me make supper tonight."

But as they ate, the girls' words reinforced what he already knew. Karen was sweet, kind and shared the same faith.

She just didn't hold the appeal she once had. Her soft green eyes and her pale blondness seemed pallid.

Pallid compared to Sandra's heavy brown hair and dancing eyes.

Chapter Six

Logan added a few more flourishes to his drawing and stood to have a better look.

His first impulse was to throw it in the garbage.

His second was to rip it up.

Then throw it in the garbage.

He wasn't exactly sure why he didn't like it, just that it looked like every other house in Calgary right now. Boxy and choppy with cluttered rooflines.

"Uncle Logan, we're done with the dishes." Bethany stood in the doorway of his office looking especially demure.

He nodded absently.

"Can me and Brittany ask you a favor?"

Logan frowned and turned, giving his niece his full attention. "Since when do you girls ask if you can ask?"

Bethany lifted her hands and shoulders at the same time, signaling complete incomprehension.

"So, what is it?"

"Well, it's Grandma's birthday pretty soon, and me and Brit want to make her a present to give to her. We wanted to give her something real special and we had a good idea."

"And what's the point of all this?" Logan asked, stifling a yawn.

"Well…" Bethany hesitated, pressing her fingers together as if in supplication. "We thought it would be fun to make a stained glass sun catcher. Sandra said she would help us."

Logan shouldn't have been surprised. Since Sunday, the girls had been jockeying to visit Sandra each evening, and each evening he firmly said no.

"It would make a real cool present for her," Bethany added.

"You girls just don't quit, do you?" he said, shaking his head.

Bethany looked the picture of innocence, and once again Logan went through all the reasons they shouldn't go to Sandra's. She was their tutor, not their friend, and it was important to teach them the difference. She was much older than them and probably not a whole lot wiser, in spite of her degree. He didn't like them hanging around with her. Period.

Although the last was becoming harder to justify. He had given her the responsibility of teaching his nieces, and in spite of their differing over her methods, the girls were understanding their work.

Brittany joined Bethany. Reinforcements, he thought wryly. "Come to add your two cents?" he asked her, his hands on his hips.

"We thought it would be a good idea to go," Brittany said, ignoring his rhetorical question. "This way you could have some more time alone to work on your project." Her eyes skittered to the drawing on his board, and her face fell. "Are you done?"

Logan didn't even bother to give the rendering another second of his attention. He sighed. "No, I'm not. I thought I was, but I don't like it."

Brittany walked to the drawing and held it up. "It looks okay," she said. "But not your best work."

Logan bit back the quick smile at Brittany's authoritative tone. She glanced at him, perfectly serious. "Looks like it's back to the drawing board."

"I guess."

"So you'll want some more quiet time," she added.

Logan couldn't stop his smile. "You're more than just a pretty face, Brittany," he said, his voice full of admiration. He knew exactly where she was headed.

"Maybe we should visit Sandra and she can help us with Grandma's birthday present so you'll have the house to yourself for a while."

Logan held their innocent gazes and against his will he had to admit that he was beat. He raised his hands as if in surrender. "Okay, okay," he said with a suppressed sigh. He crossed his arms over his chest and looked first at one, then the other. "I will bring you girls there and come and pick you up at exactly nine o'clock. Sharp. No excuses."

"Okay," they said in unison.

"Can we go now?" Bethany asked.

Once he had caved in, he couldn't think of a reason.

Logan glanced at his watch. Eight-eighteen. Still too early to go and get the girls. When he had dropped them off at Sandra's place, she'd been cool and reserved. Just as she'd been when she came to work with the girls during the day. They spent as much time outside as possible, as if avoiding him. They went for short walks into the hills and came back giggling and laughing. When, out of curiosity, he asked her what she was doing, she told him, but her tone was defensive. He didn't like it.

Sighing, he picked up his pencil, made a few half-hearted doodles and glared at the result. This project was slowly losing its appeal, even though he couldn't put it out of his head. Sure, it would be nice to get the Jonserads as clients, but this project was starting to consume him. He found no joy in it. And, he reminded himself, it wasn't even a sure thing.

He got up from his makeshift drawing board and wandered to the living room.

He tried to analyze the peculiar restlessness that had gripped him since Sunday. He was sure it wasn't Karen. When she left he had felt relief more than anything. But she was a reminder to him of what he had once had. A girlfriend. Someone who cared that he was spending his entire holiday on a project when he really should be sitting at the beach with his nieces.

She was also a reminder of his one-time freedom and the chance to make choices for himself. No responsibilities other than his own.

Since the girls had come into his life, he felt a keen pressure to provide for them, to make sure that they had food and clothes and that their schoolwork was done. To supervise them and to seek out their best interests.

He thought of Sandra again and begrudgingly realized that with her the girls were enthusiastic and did their work. He wondered what they were doing right now.

A quick glance at his watch showed him that precisely sixty seconds had passed. He dropped into his recliner and, pushing the papers he had been reading aside, he reached for his Bible. Yesterday was the last time he had read it, and in his current frame of mind, he needed the comfort he knew he would find there.

Leafing through the pages, he found the Psalm he had often read to the girls when they first came. Psalm sixty-eight. "Sing to God, sing praise to His name, extol Him who rides on the clouds—His name is the Lord—and rejoice before Him. A father to the fatherless, a defender of widows, is God in His holy dwelling. God sets the lonely in families, He leads forth the prisoners with singing."

Logan smiled as he read the familiar words. When the girls came to his home, they were lonely, grieving and afraid. They knew him, but just in passing, and now they were living with him.

Bethany and Brittany had been comforted by the words and comforted by the faith they were slowly discovering each day.

A faith he tried to nurture wherever possible. He had found a Christian school they could attend. He took them to church, got them involved in the youth group. Each day he tried, in his own inadequate way, to show them God's love.

So how did someone like Sandra fit into their lives? She didn't go to church, though she professed a faith in God. How wise was it to let her teach girls who were still struggling in their own faith?

Logan's second thoughts made him close the Bible and get up. It didn't matter what time he had told the girls he was going to pick them up, he was leaving now.

The streets of Elkwater were quiet as he made his way to Sandra's place. From a distance he heard the insistent boom of a stereo. Probably some teenagers whooping it up on the campground, he figured. He felt sorry for the campers. At least he didn't have to contend with that, because they owned their own cabin.

The lights were on in Sandra's house, and he realized that the music he had thought was coming from the campground was coming from Sandra's stereo.

He knocked on the door, knowing it was futile over the noise. So he let himself in.

When he had dropped the girls off, Sandra had been sitting outside reading, so he hadn't gone in. He stepped into the house, curiously glancing around at the array of mismatched furniture, the books piled on every available table. It was neat, sort of, yet with a lived-in and comfortable feeling. The lighting in this part of the house was warm, created by the jeweled glow of two stained glass lamps—a tall standing lamp hovering behind a well-worn chair and a table lamp across the room. Sandra's creations, he presumed.

"Hello," he called, staying in the entrance. The music was coming from a room off the living room. He waited, then Bethany popped her head around the corner.

"Oh, hi, Uncle Logan," she called.

"Don't sound so excited to see me," he returned with a grin.

The music was turned down, and Sandra appeared behind Bethany, glancing at her watch.

"I know. I'm early," he said. "I just thought I'd see what the girls were up to."

"Checking on me?" Sandra asked with a petulant tilt of her eyebrows.

"Nope, just bored."

Sandra angled her head toward the room they had come out of. "Come in, then, and see what they've been doing."

Logan forced a smile, wondering again why she was so cool in his presence. Wondering why he didn't like it.

He followed Sandra into a brightly lit room, watching as she walked to the stereo and turned it down more.

"Sorry about that. The girls brought some CDs. I told them they could play them while we worked." She shoved her hands in the back pockets of her jeans, tossing her hair behind her shoulders. "It's Christian music, in case you were wondering."

Logan felt the defensiveness in her attitude. He was at a loss as to what caused it. "That's fine," he said quietly.

The girls were bent over a table, pretending not to watch Logan and Sandra. Logan walked to them, glancing over their shoulders. All he saw was an array of pieces of glass, some edged with what looked like thin strips of copper. "So what is this?"

Brittany looked at Sandra. "I'll make lemonade and you tell Uncle Logan what we're doing. You know it better anyway." She turned to her sister. "C'mon, Bethy, lets go."

The two girls fled. Logan shrugged in Sandra's direction, hoping she understood what the girls were up to. "I guess it's up to you," he said with a forced smile.

Sandra blew out her breath and walked to his side, keeping her distance, as if reluctant to come too close. "They're making a sun catcher. Here's the pattern." She pointed out a stylized black-and-white sketch of an iris in an oval frame. "They have to trace the pattern pieces on the glass and then cut them with this cutter." She held up a small, pencil-shaped object. "After grinding the edges they have to foil each piece. Then dab kester on it to get rid of the finish. After that they solder it together."

Logan nodded, pretending to understand.

Sandra glanced his way, and their gazes meshed. She curled one corner of her mouth, showing the first semblance of a smile since Sunday. "You don't have a clue what I'm talking about, do you?"

"I got foiled by the foil."

She held his gaze, and her smile grew. "I see."

So once again she explained the process, showing him how the individual pieces of glass were wrapped in foil that was sticky on one side. "You have to make sure you go all around and that you give enough foil on each side of the glass," she explained, showing him.

Logan stepped a little closer, ostensibly to see what she was showing him. But as he did, he caught the faint scent of her perfume—light, fresh and lingering. It caught him unexpectedly. Made him pause and breathe a little more deeply.

"Once all the pieces are wrapped, you have to lay it out in the same shape as the pattern," she continued, oblivious to the reaction she had elicited in him. "This is when you need the kester, a type of acid, to get rid of the finish on the foil so that the solder can stick to it. I don't have the soldering iron plugged in because we're not ready yet." She reached across the table, picked up a small project she had been working on and set it in front of Logan without looking at him.

He glanced at her hands, stained and marked with small white scars. From handling glass, he presumed. Hands that carefully handled the piece she held.

"This is what it should look like when it's done. The solder should lie in a nice, neat bead on both sides of the work. It gives the same effect as lead but without the weight."

"Can I?" Logan reached out for the sun catcher she was holding, and with a shrug Sandra handed it to him. Their fingers brushed each other, sending a peculiar riffle up his arm at the contact.

He forced his attention to what he held, astonished at how small some of the pieces of glass were, how intricately she had cut them and put them all together. When he held it up to the light, it was as if it came to life.

"This is amazing. I'm guessing you did the lamps in the living room, as well."

She nodded, stepping back from him, taking that beguiling scent with her.

"Do you do other work besides this?"

"I've done some windows. But I use lead for them. A slightly different process."

"For homes?"

"No. Churches."

Logan couldn't resist. "Oh. For those hypocrites," he teased.

She held his gaze, smiling. "It's all for the glory of God," she returned.

Logan didn't look away. Didn't want to. He felt his smile fade as he tried to delve into her deep brown eyes, tried to find something solid, something serious behind her flippant facade.

"And do you think He's glorified?" he asked quietly.

Sandra looked away, then shrugged. "I guess you'll have to ask Him sometime," she said.

Logan recognized the retreat and decided to leave it at that. "Do you support yourself doing this?"

Sandra rolled her shoulders in answer. "I don't have high needs. But I've got a contract with a restaurant in Calgary to supply them with some lamps. I'm pretty pleased about that."

"Have you started on them yet?" He laid the piece down and glanced at her again.

She shook her head. "I've been busy with the girls...." She let the sentence drift off as she retreated one more step. "I should see how they're doing."

Logan watched her go, wondering once again at her sudden reticence.

* * *

"Tastes just about right," Sandra said, taking a sip of the lemonade the girls offered her. "Why don't you get your uncle Logan and tell him that it's ready?"

Bethany ran out of the small kitchen as Brittany set out four cups. "Do you have any cookies?" Brittany asked as she filled the cups. "They would go really nice with lemonade."

"No. Sorry." Sandra flashed her an apologetic grin. "I'm a little low on cookies right now." Low on groceries, period. Thanks to Cora, who consumed gallons of lemonade, she at least had lemonade crystals.

She bit her lip as she stirred the lemonade, wondering if she could work up enough courage to ask Logan for an advance.

And what would he think of her if he found out how tight things actually were for her? These days, her idea of a seven-course meal was stopping outside the restaurant in town and taking a deep sniff.

Luckily utilities were included with the cottage rent, which had been paid in advance, or the roof over her head might have been iffy, as well. Logan's low opinion of her would sink if he knew the particulars of her financial situation.

She had tried to tell herself that what he thought of her didn't matter. But after meeting Karen—after seeing a perfectly put together woman who probably phoned home once a week, who attended church with Logan and the girls, who probably never had an unsuitable boyfriend—Sandra had spent the past few days feeling less confident than normal.

Which was annoying, of course. Self-confidence wasn't something Sandra usually lacked.

She looked up as Logan and the girls came into the kitchen.

"Why are you still stirring that?" Bethany asked.

"It takes a lot of stirring," Sandra said quickly to cover up. "I'm hoping to carbonate it." She grinned, then put out the four cups and motioned for everyone to sit down.

"Can we go back and work on the sun catcher?" Brittany picked up her cup and tugged on her sister's arm with her free hand.

Sandra glanced at Logan, who was sitting down. His face didn't change expression.

"I think you girls can stay here with us," he commented, taking a sip of his lemonade.

"Well, we want to get it done." Brittany gave Bethany's arm another tug. Without looking at Logan, they left.

Sandra gave Logan a forced grin. "Well, here we are. Alone again." Goodness, she thought. If that didn't sound like a proposition. She felt like smacking herself on the forehead.

"Sorry about that." Logan scratched his forehead with his index finger as if trying to puzzle out his nieces. "Tact isn't a word that comes to mind when one thinks of Brittany and Bethany." He sighed lightly. "I'd like to think that they might be a little less subtle, but I guess I misplaced that part of the training manual."

Sandra couldn't help but smile at his deprecating humor. "You've done well with them. In spite of missing parts of the course."

Logan looked at her as if puzzled by her compliment. "Thanks, I think."

His moment of vulnerability was surprisingly captivating. In spite of her resolve to keep her distance from this man, she found she wanted to reassure him. "Really, Logan. They're nice girls, and I know they think very highly of you."

Logan's deep hazel eyes met and held hers. His face relaxed, a shifting of his features, and Sandra felt herself drawn to him. Unable to look away.

"That's good to know," he said, taking a sip of his lemonade and setting the cup down. "There are many times that I feel like all I'm doing is damage control. Just trying to catch up. That's life, I guess."

"Life is hard. You get the test first, the lessons later," Sandra mused, quirking him a grin.

He angled his head, as if to look at her from a different perspective. "You always have a quick comeback, don't you?"

"Mind like a steel trap," she quipped, uncomfortable with his scrutiny. "Except it's rusty and illegal in most parts of the country."

Logan didn't respond, merely leaned his elbows on the table as he continued to look at her. "So what makes you tick, Sandra Bachman?" He held up his hand as if to stop her. "Okay, that was giving you a wide-open opportunity. Let me try that again with a more specific question. How did you get here? To Elkwater?"

Sandra wondered at his sudden interest. Wondered what he would say were she to tell him the facts of her life. Facts that would only reinforce his opinion of her.

She looked at her cup, ran her thumbnail along an old scratch in the plastic and decided to be honest. His opinion couldn't get much lower, she figured. "I came here from Vancouver Island. Actually, Hornby Island. Cora, the woman I rent this house with, and I met up there. We both decided we'd had enough of the life there and wandered around until we stumbled on this place."

"What did you do on Hornby Island?"

"Stained glass work. Like I'm doing now."

"Did you make a living at it?"

Sandra pressed her thumbnail a little harder into the scratch, biting her lip. "Sort of."

"Do you enjoy it?"

Sandra hesitated. She had. At one time. It was something new and interesting. And totally different from what her father would approve of.

The thought plucked at her with nervous fingers. Was that her only reason for doing it? To make her father angry?

She dismissed the questions and their nugget of truth.

"I like it," she admitted. "Usually."

"Just like? Is there anything you love doing?"

Sandra frowned at him. "What is this? Part of my ongoing interview?"

"Maybe," Logan admitted. "But I'm also curious."

He caught her eye as he leaned forward, as if inviting her confidence.

Sandra felt an ache grow. In spite of their earlier antagonism, she sensed his interest and wondered again about Karen.

"I like doing a lot of things," Sandra admitted, not moving from her position.

"Why didn't you ever use your teaching degree?"

Sandra glanced at him. Logan's mouth curled at one corner in a smile that created a dimple in his cheek.

She tried to find the words to explain the heavy weight of responsibility that dogged her all through school, through college. The feeling that no matter how hard she tried, she never measured up. Would Logan, with his easygoing upbringing, even have the faintest notion of how debilitating the unceasing expectations of her parents could be?

She thought of Florence Napier, remembered comments Logan made about his upbringing and what he wanted for his nieces. She remembered Florence's laissez-faire attitude.

He wouldn't understand, she thought.

"Teaching wasn't what I really wanted to do," she said, settling on a mundane answer as she leaned back in her chair.

"You're good at it."

"Thanks. But two girls as opposed to a whole classroom of kids..." She shrugged. "Not my style, I'm afraid."

"Why not?"

Sandra felt herself stiffen at the tone of his question. "Not everyone is cut out for that kind of thing."

"Meaning?"

"Routine. Schedule. The same thing every day."

Logan held her gaze, his expression unreadable.

"That's not your style," he replied quietly.

"No, it isn't," she answered with a little more force than the comment required.

"What would be your ideal job, then?"

Sandra looked away, pulling the corner of her lower lip between her teeth. She wasn't sure. She had spent so much time figuring out what she didn't want to do that she hadn't formulated a clear plan of what she did want. The past few years had been a whirl of trying and discarding.

"I'm sure your girlfriend Karen is the kind of person who has her life all figured out. I'm not like that."

Logan tipped his eyebrows. "She's not my girlfriend."

Why did that simple statement ease a small measure of the loneliness that had gripped her on Sunday?

"I...I'm not sure what my ideal job would be," Sandra said quickly, looking away. "I haven't found it yet."

"That's too bad, Sandra. I think you have a lot of potential."

Then, taking a final sip of his lemonade, he got up. He set his cup down, hooked his thumbs in the tops of his pants pockets, one corner of his mouth caught between his teeth. He looked as if he wanted to say something else. "Thanks for the lemonade." He tilted her a halfhearted grin and went to the back room to get the girls.

Sandra hugged herself, watching him go, wondering why she had said what she did. It was as if she was determined to keep him at arm's length.

And she should. *He's an architect,* she reminded

herself. *A secure, solid, hardworking architect who lives for schedules and routine.*

A man who took good care of the women in his life—his nieces, his mother.

A man who probably would never do to Karen what Henri had done to her, she thought with a faint feeling of remorse.

And in spite of his comment about Karen, a man who would be out of her life once they all went back to Calgary, she reminded herself. She and Logan moved in different circles. Only for this moment had their lives intersected.

The girls gave her noisy goodbyes as they left. Logan ushered them out the door. In the doorway he turned to face her. "Thanks for working with them tonight." Still holding on to the door, his eyes met hers.

Once again, Sandra had that peculiar feeling of an intangible allurement that tightened between them, drawing her toward him.

She looked away and nodded. Her only reply.

The door closed, and Sandra was alone again. As she heard the girls' excited chatter and Logan's deep voice fading away, it was as if the house had grown smaller, emptier.

Restless, Sandra got up, went to the stereo and turned it up. Unfamiliar music spilled out of the speakers. Bethany's CD, Sandra remembered. She was about to turn it down but was stopped by the music. Upbeat and catchy. She found herself tapping her fingers against her leg in time to the beat.

The singer sang the words with an absoluteness that

Sandra would once have dismissed as narrow-minded, but the sincerity in her voice kept Sandra from turning the song off.

In the lyrics of the song Sandra heard a call back to the faith of her youth, a call to come and worship Jesus as Lord, a challenge that one day every tongue would confess God, every knee would bow.

Sandra felt a shiver of apprehension followed by a pressing of guilt and sorrow as the music swelled, built in intensity, the singer drawing Sandra in.

She felt a touch of God's hand. Just like she did when she was outside, when she looked into the heavens and knew for certainty that the vastness and the order she saw there didn't come through happenstance.

She hit the power button and turned the music off. Standing alone in the empty room, Sandra closed her eyes as the now familiar loneliness washed over her.

Home, she thought. She wished she could go home.

But that was out of the question.

"He hasn't kissed her yet," Brittany whispered to her sister, setting the plates on the table.

Bethany spun around, still holding the utensils she had pulled out of the drawer. "How do you know?"

Brittany glanced over her shoulder and tiptoed to the door. But Uncle Logan was still in the shower.

"I watched them last night. They were just sitting and talking." She shook her head in disgust. "This is taking forever."

Bethany carefully set the knives beside the plates Brittany had laid out. "We just have to wait, I guess."

"I wish I knew if that Karen was going to come back."

Bethany shuddered. "She really likes Uncle Logan. I wish she'd leave him alone."

"Well, I don't think he likes her much. He never even held her hand when they were walking."

"So we have to keep getting Sandra and Uncle Logan together," said Bethany with a sigh. "We don't have much longer."

"Good morning, girls," Logan said from the doorway, toweling his wet hair. "You're up bright and early."

Brittany threw Bethany a guilty look, wondering if Uncle Logan had heard what they said. She looked at him, smiling, hoping he didn't. "Just thought we'd get up early so we can do some schoolwork."

Logan paused, holding the towel, looking at Brittany as if he didn't quite believe her. "You're doing homework in the morning?"

Brittany nodded. "Sandra gave us a contest. She said if we get our work done by tonight, she was going to take us out to look at the meteor shower." She stopped. "Oops. I wasn't supposed to tell you."

"You weren't?" Logan hung on to his towel, his dark eyes flicking over one, then the other twin. "Why not?"

"I think it was a secret," Brittany said, biting her lip.

Logan nodded once, then left.

"Do you think he was mad?" Bethany asked, her eyes wide. "He sounded mad."

Brittany shrugged. "I hope not. Otherwise Sandra might get in trouble with him again."

Logan stood by the window watching as Sandra came up the road to the cabin, her knapsack slung over one shoulder, her hands shoved in the pockets of her faded blue jeans. She wore her hair back, tied in a heavy braid that hung over one shoulder.

She looked much younger than he knew her to be. More like an older sister of his nieces than their tutor.

Mentally he compared her to Karen, whose clothing was always up to date, polished.

Once he had envisioned Karen as a potential wife, the perfect complement to an up-and-coming architect.

But after seeing Karen on Sunday and spending time with her again, he knew that even though she seemed more than willing to come back to him, he wasn't ready to take her. Nothing in his circumstances had changed. He still had the girls, and she still wasn't comfortable around them.

Whereas Sandra had an ease and naturalness that he admired, in spite of questionable characteristics that he didn't. Like keeping tonight's excursion a big secret from him.

As Sandra came up the wooden sidewalk to the cabin, Logan stepped away from the window hoping she hadn't seen him. When she knocked on the door, he was already there, opening it for her.

She looked taken aback at the sight of him, then recovered. "Hey, there. How are you?" she asked, stepping past him. "The girls ready for another day of education?"

Logan nodded, wondering how he was going to approach her. It seemed that just as one thing was resolved between them, something else came up.

He decided to go straight to it.

"Brittany told me about your plans to see the meteor shower tonight."

Sandra nodded, shrugging her knapsack off her shoulder. "That's right."

"She said that you had asked her not to tell me. I'd like to know why you don't think I need to be consulted about this."

Sandra let the knapsack drop with a muffled thud and looked directly at him, all traces of good humor vanished. "Is this going to go on until I'm done, Logan Napier?" she asked, her voice chilled. "This constant questioning and mistrusting and wondering if I'm good enough?" She began pulling books out of her backpack, her movements jerky with anger. "I'm taking my job with them very seriously." She slammed a book on the table. "I'm not some heathen that is determined to turn your nieces astray. They're learning things and I'm doing a good job." Another book joined the first with a heavy thump. She threw a fistful of pencils on the table.

Logan watched her sudden spill of anger, heard the indignation in her voice. It seemed out of proportion to what he had asked her, and for a moment he wondered what was behind her anger. He forced his mind to the topic at hand.

"You have to admit, Sandra, I have a right to know what's happening," he said quietly, leaning against the door. "All I ask is that you let me know."

Sandra's gaze flew to his, her dark eyes snapping with suppressed indignation. She blinked, then looked at the books on the table. "I'm sorry," she said, straightening them, tidying the pencils. She took a slow breath, pulling her hands over her face as if to erase the anger he had seen etched there a moment ago. "I told Brittany not to say anything so that I could ask you. I wasn't trying to hide anything from you. I was going to ask you last night, but I forgot."

She stood by the table, looking straight ahead, avoiding his gaze. "I'm sorry that you thought that of me."

Logan felt a flicker of guilt mixed with sympathy for her and wondered once again at the mystery that eddied around her. He walked to her side and gently laid his hand on her shoulder, feeling the warmth of her skin through the thin T-shirt she wore. "I'm sorry, too, Sandra," he said. "I guess I just jumped to the wrong conclusion."

"You seem to do that often." She looked at him, her chin up.

"I know." Logan squeezed her shoulder. He told himself it was his way of apologizing, but he enjoyed the brief contact too much for that. He had to resist the urge to let his hand linger, to toy with the hank of hair that lay inches from his hand.

He stepped back, momentarily shaken by his feelings.

"So when do you plan on doing this?" he asked, hoping his voice sounded normal.

"I thought we could go out tonight." Sandra angled him a quick look over her shoulder. Their eyes held a moment, and Logan found himself unable to break the brief contact.

"I was going to walk to the hill behind your cabin. There's a better place farther along, but it's not within walking distance." She returned his smile, and Logan felt a faint twist in his midsection.

He nodded, picking up on her vaguely worded hint. "In other words, you need a vehicle."

She nodded, then to his surprise said, "But you can come along if you want."

"That would be nice," he said, their gazes still locked.

Then she looked away, breaking the insidious connection, leaving Logan to wonder if she was as shaken at the contact as he had been.

Chapter Seven

"**W**hy did you ask him to come?" Sandra muttered to herself, hunching her shoulders deeper in the light jacket she had thrown on. She strode down the darkened streets to the Napier cabin. "He's pushy and he'll only criticize what you do." But even as she tried to list all the reasons she shouldn't have asked Logan along, she knew there were deeper reasons. Reasons she didn't want to delve too far into for fear of making them too real.

She was becoming attracted to Logan Napier.

Sandra stopped, biting her lip as she considered her position. She could cancel. She could turn around and change her mind. It was, after all, one-thirty in the morning. Surely they wouldn't mind missing out.

But Sandra had promised the girls this event as a reward for all their hard work during the week, and they were looking forward to it with an amazing amount of enthusiasm. She didn't think girls the age of Bethany and Brittany would be interested in meteor showers. Asking Logan along had been a silly impulse. This morning, when he had put his hand on her shoulder, it was as if every nerve in her body swung like a compass needle toward his touch.

She couldn't imagine why one simple gesture from a guy like Logan could turn her knees to jelly.

But it had, and afterward, when she could analyze it, she knew that spending time with him was just playing with fire. He wasn't her type—he'd drive her crazy in a week. And if she fell in love with him...

"Whoa, whoa, now you're really jumping the gun," she said. She shook her head as if to dislodge even the faintest mote of the previous idea.

Sandra bit her lip, still hesitating. Then, laughing at her foolishness, she walked on. Logan was here temporarily. Once he was gone, her life could go back to, well, whatever it should be.

She bounded up the steps and knocked on the door of the darkened house. No answer. A quick glance at her watch told her that she was right on time.

Just as she was about to knock again, the door opened, and the light in the cabin was turned on, throwing out rectangles of golden yellow on the lawn.

Framed by the door, backlit by the light in the cabin, stood Logan.

His hair was unkempt, and whiskers stubbled his firm jaw, accenting the slight indentation in its center. His eyes were bleary with sleep. He was dressed, however, in a wrinkled T-shirt and jeans. No khaki pants tonight.

"Hi there," he said, his voice still husky from disuse. Sandra felt a peculiar little thrill at the sound.

"I'm not early, am I?" she said quickly.

Logan yawned, scratching his chin. His fingers rasped over his whiskers. "Nope." He glanced at Sandra, blinking. "How do you manage to look so perky at this ridiculous time of night?"

Sandra shrugged, warmed at the offhand compliment. "I don't need much sleep."

Logan yawned again. "Lucky you. Well, come in. The girls are just getting ready."

Sandra stepped inside. Logan closed the door behind her and ambled toward the kitchen.

He stumbled, muttered something under his breath and stood for a moment, glaring at the offending table.

Sandra stifled a laugh at the sight and was rewarded with a bleary look from Logan.

"Sorry," she said, with a quick shrug of her shoulders.

"I somehow doubt that," he replied. But his grin belied the gruffness of his voice.

"We're ready to go," Brittany called, stepping out of the kitchen.

"So am I," Sandra said. "Now we just have to get your uncle Logan ready."

She glanced pointedly at Logan's bare feet. He stared at her as if he didn't understand, then looked down. "Oops. Sorry." He yawned again, trudged to his bedroom and came back a few minutes later holding his shoes.

Rubbing his eyes, he sat in the nearest chair, dropped his shoes on the floor and stared into space.

Sandra waited for him to put his shoes on. But he didn't move.

"Logan?" she asked, taking a step nearer. She glanced at the girls, who merely lifted their shoulders in puzzlement.

"Hey, let's get going." She reached out, grasped his shoulder and gave it a little shake.

He blinked, then, looking at her, smiled. It was a smile with no reservation, a smile that held no hint of his usual asperity. "Hi, Sandra," he said, his voice husky, lowered to an intimate level. Then, to her surprise, he lifted his hand, resting it on hers. His hand was large, engulfing hers, his fingers warm as they lightly caressed her own.

Sandra swallowed as her heart rate jumped. She pulled her hand back as if burned. "Logan? Are you awake?"

He blinked, frowned, then blinked again, and Sandra realized with a beat of disappointment that he hadn't been.

"What's up?" he asked, looking around, puzzled, completely unaware of what had just happened.

"It's time to go," Sandra said stiffly, grasping her knapsack strap with both hands.

"Okay." He nodded and slipped on his shoes. As he bent to tie them, Sandra looked away, directly into the smirking faces of the twins.

"Well, girls," she said briskly, covering her confusion, "get your things together and we'll leave."

"We have everything, Sandra," Bethany said, still grinning.

"Good. That's good." Sandra took a step back as Logan stood up and blinked. He looked at her as if seeing her for the first time. A frown wrinkled his fore-head then he shook his head lightly and turned away.

"I'll go start the van," he said, slipping on a denim jacket.

Sandra nodded. She avoided meeting his eyes, wondering if he had truly forgotten what he had done.

The drive through the hills would have been silent if it had depended on Logan or Sandra to make conversation. Fortunately the girls had more than enough to talk about. They asked Sandra questions about what they were going to see, even though they knew.

"I can't guarantee we're going to see a lot of meteor activity," Sandra said as Logan parked the van at the top of the hill on a graveled turnout. "But from what I know, this is an ideal time."

"One-thirty in the morning is anything but ideal," Logan muttered, getting out of the van.

"Hey, you didn't have to come." Sandra angled him a quick glance.

In the reflected glow of the van's headlights, Sandra caught his eye, and she once again remembered the feel of his hand on hers. She looked away.

"C'mon, girls, get the stuff we'll need and then we can get this show on the road," she said.

Sandra pulled her sweater closer around her. The daytime temperatures were hot, but in the open prairie, the middle of the night was always cool.

"Where do you want us to be?" Logan asked, carrying the blanket that Sandra had taken along.

"I'd like to go just beyond the gravel. The hill is open to the south, and I'd like to face that direction."

Sandra led the way, the beams from the van illuminating her path through the brush.

They came to an open hillside, protected from a faint breeze by the trees that fanned out on either side.

"Perfect," Sandra said with satisfaction. "Okay, girls. Lay out your bags right here."

"I'll go and shut off the van's headlights," Logan offered, handing Sandra the blanket. Her eyes were still semiblinded by the van's lights, so she couldn't see his expression. He waited a moment, then turned and left.

"Here, girls, help me lay out this blanket," she said to the girls, pulling herself into the moment. *Concentrate, concentrate,* she thought.

She wished she hadn't asked him along. It was going to be an awkward event.

"We remembered our flashlights and pens and paper," Bethany offered as they laid the blanket out.

"Good for you. I'm hoping we'll see a lot of meteors right now."

A rustle in the bushes brought her senses to alert, then she realized it was Logan coming back from the van, and she felt even more tense.

Her eyes were slowly becoming adjusted to the dark, and she felt a sense of déjà vu. Remembered another time he had materialized out of the darkness.

Sandra turned quickly to the girls and sat on one edge of the blanket, indicating that they were to sit beside her.

"What is the name of the meteor shower we're going to watch?" she asked, putting on her teacher's voice as she tried not to notice Logan sitting down just a few feet away.

"The Phoenicids," both girls replied.

"Good. So why are we up this early in the morning to watch them?"

"Because the moon is gone now," Bethany said, stifling a yawn. "And the sky is as dark as it is going to be."

"And what is the moon called?"

Silence greeted that question.

"The moon," Brittany said, puzzled.

"A gibbous moon. Another word for the shape of the moon." Sandra pulled out her book of star charts as she spoke. "And what's another reason we're up at this ridiculous time?"

Silence again.

Sandra was disappointed that they hadn't remembered what she had shown them this afternoon. It didn't speak well for her training, and some perverse part of her was trying to show Logan what a good teacher she was.

Then Brittany rescued her. "I think I remember. Is it because we're facing the same way the earth is traveling in the orbit?" Sandra could hear the question in her voice. "You said something about snow and snowflakes and driving."

"Very good." Sandra felt a surge of relief. "If we're facing in any other direction, it's like looking out of the back window of a van during a snowstorm. You'll see some meteors, but not as much as if you're in the front of the van. Right now we're heading into the meteor shower, like a van into a snowstorm." She went on to show the girls where in the sky was the best place to look. Flashlights came out, and they bent over the book.

"Uncle Logan, come and see, too," Brittany ordered. And Uncle Logan obediently got up from his side of the blanket and looked over Sandra's shoulder.

She tried to concentrate on what she was showing the girls, but all her senses were alert to his presence behind her.

Luckily it was dark, and the girls were bent over the book, pointing out the constellations.

"Okay, get out your pens and paper and be sure to notice where you see meteors, how long you see them and keep a note of the time between them."

The flashlights were shut off, and the little group was plunged into darkness.

Slowly, as Sandra's night vision righted itself, she could better make out the figures of the girls lying down on the blanket beside her and Logan, who sat behind them.

She hugged her knees, looking at the sky. She knew she was going to get a sore neck if she stayed in this position, but she was certainly not going to lie down. Not with Logan so close behind her.

"There's one," Brittany said, pointing up.

"Mark it down," Sandra prompted. "But try to write without the flashlight so your eyes don't have to get used to the dark again."

She heard their pens scratching on the paper.

"So how did you know when the shower was coming?" Logan asked from behind her.

"Earth intersects these meteoroid swarms at about the same relative time and place each year," Sandra said confidently, clutching her knees. She was on familiar territory here.

"And where does the name come from?"

"When we cross one of these swarms, the meteors seem to come from a common point of origin, known as a radiant. This regular shower is named after the constellation from which it seems to originate."

He was quiet again. Then he got up and stretched out on the other side of Brittany. Sandra ruthlessly suppressed a twinge of disappointment. Crazy. That's what it was.

Or maybe just plain loneliness, another voice said.

Sandra pressed her chin against her knees, staring at the stars that went directly to the horizon, meeting the faint outline of the hills that sloped away from them. Sitting outside under the stars always made her feel vulnerable and philosophical.

The lines of her life had, of late, not fallen in pleasant places. She thought that her hard-won freedom would have given her a sense of satisfaction. Instead it was as if each move was a move away from something rather than a move toward something.

She glanced past the girls at Logan, who lay on the blanket, his hand under his head. He seemed to know what he wanted and how to go about getting it. In spite of his interference, or maybe because of it, she realized that he was a concerned uncle. She wondered how many of the men she had met in her life would willingly take in two young girls, thereby risking their own freedom.

She sighed lightly, her gaze falling on the girls who were watching her watching Logan.

She looked away.

"How many have you seen, Bethany?" she asked, disconcerted that they had caught her staring at their uncle.

"Four already."

"Good for you." She lay back, watching the sky, reminding herself of the reason she was here. The girls first and foremost.

"The stars sure are peaceful," Logan said quietly. "Unchanging. Always the same. Amazing."

A few moments before, Sandra might have agreed with him, but her reactions to him left her feeling edgy.

"Actually they aren't," she contradicted. "Out there are colliding neutron stars, gamma ray bursts, black holes. All kinds of noise and confusion."

"What's a gamma ray?" Bethany asked.

"A powerful form of light. More energetic than a microwave or X-ray. Like the difference between humming and screaming." She stopped herself, knowing she was spouting off. Knowing that if she kept talking she would end up talking above the girls' heads.

"Can you see gamma rays?"

"No. Not with the naked eye."

"Then what's the point?" Bethany asked.

"I think God made some things just for His own pleasure," Sandra said. "We can't even see the tiniest amount of all the stars and galaxies He made, but He still made them."

"You believe in God?" Bethany asked.

"Of course, I do." Sandra wondered where that question had come from and wondered if that explained part of Logan's reserve with her. "How can you look up at all of this and not believe that it was created by God?''

"Cool."

"Really cool." Brittany sat up, shivering. "I'm cold, Sandra. I want my sweater." She stood and grabbed her sister's hand. "C'mon, Bethy, I'm scared in the dark. You come with me."

Sandra could see Logan lift himself onto his elbow. "Do you want me to come?" he asked.

"No. That's okay, Uncle Logan." As they walked through the bushes, Sandra could hear faint giggles and wondered what they were up to.

But Logan lay down, seemingly unconcerned.

"You seem to know a lot about astronomy," he commented.

Sandra shrugged, sitting up. "When I graduated from high school, my first choice was to go into that field."

"Why didn't you?"

Sandra hugged her knees. "My parents wanted me to study something that would give me a job at the end. And since they were paying for my education..."

"You took teaching." Logan finished the sentence for her.

"Bingo."

She heard as much as saw, in her peripheral vision, Logan sit up, leaning on one elbow again. "Why didn't you go ahead? On your own?"

She thought back to that time. To the daily confrontations she had with her father over her education, her mother hovering, always the peacemaker. Except there never was any peace to make between Sandra and her father. There was always something to fight about. Her clothes, her friends, her marks. Always something that didn't measure up.

The memories dredged up old feelings of inadequacy. She turned to Logan, finding her own questions. "Did *you* go it on your own?"

Logan laughed lightly. "Absolutely. I paid my own way. I got where I did by the grace of God and my own hard work."

"With no help from your parents?"

"Sandra, you know what my mother is like. We lived hand to mouth as long as I can remember. One of the benefits of living a free and easy life."

Sandra pulled her lip between her teeth as she thought of her financial situation, also the result of the free and easy life Logan spoke disparagingly of. "Money isn't everything," she said softly, trying to find some feeble way of justifying her choices.

Logan was quiet. In the dark, all she could see of him was the gleam of his eyes, then a flash of white as he grinned.

"Is that the best you can do, Sandra? 'Money isn't everything.' I expected better."

She couldn't stop her answering smile. "Sorry. I must be a little off my form tonight."

Logan sat up and faced her, sitting cross-legged. "So what made you interested in astronomy?"

Thankfully he had found another topic. Talking about her parents always created a mixture of guilt, anger and frustration.

"I guess I was drawn to the vastness of this universe. The fact that there is so much dark interspersed with so much light. That during the day, light is stronger, then in the evening, darkness wins out.''

"But even in the darkest night, like now, there's light."

"And Jesus said, 'I am the light of the world,'" Sandra quoted softly.

"How about this one from Job. 'What is the way to the abode of light? And where does darkness reside?'"

Sandra paused, letting the words take root. "I've never read that before. That's beautiful."

"It's from God's mighty challenge to Job, asking him who he possibly thinks he is." Logan moved closer, creating an intimacy. "You know your Bible, Sandra, yet you claim to not need God."

"I've never made that claim," she said quietly, her heart stepping up its rhythm at his nearness. "I just don't feel that I need to restrict myself to worshiping Him in church."

"Those hypocrites," he said, his voice holding a faint teasing note.

"I only said that once."

"But you meant it?"

Sandra shrugged. She didn't know what she meant anymore. Didn't know what she needed. Since she left home, her life had lost a center, a focus. No one had challenged her on her faith until now. Until the girls. Until Logan.

"What do you really want from God, Sandra? From life?"

"Why do you want to know?" she countered, uncomfortable with his probing questions. He sounded like her father.

"I'm not sure," he whispered. To her utter surprise, he took her hand in his, stroking her fingers. "I'm not sure at all."

She looked at their connected hands, knowing she should pull away, yet unwilling to. It had been so long since she had allowed any man to get close to her. That the first man since Henri should be someone like her father...

She stopped that thought, knowing that in spite of some similarities, it wasn't really true.

"You don't like answering questions, do you, Sandra," he said, letting go of her hand.

"I've answered enough in my life," she retorted.

To her relief, Logan leaned back again, creating a distance. "From who?"

"My father."

"What was he like?"

Sandra sighed as the conversation came full circle. "I don't talk about my parents much." In the first place, none of the people she had lived with or spent time with since she left home had ever asked her about them. Second, each time she thought of them she faced a combination of emotions. Guilt and sorrow.

She suddenly realized that they had been alone a while. As she and Logan had been talking, she had heard Bethany and Brittany's faint giggling, but it had been quiet for some time now. "Where are the girls?"

Logan didn't seem too concerned. "I'm pretty sure they're not far. Brit, Bethy, where are you two scalawags?" he called.

But all that came back was silence.

Logan got to his feet, and as he did, he held out his

hand to Sandra to help her up. The gesture was casually intimate. It bespoke of established relationships and had a chivalry that Sandra had never seen before.

She couldn't stop herself from putting her hand in his, from allowing his to grip hers as he pulled her to her feet.

As soon as she was upright, however, she pulled her hand free and walked down the path, through the shrubs and to the road to the van.

The girls weren't there, either.

"Brittany, Bethany," Logan called, turning around.

He sighed, plowing his hand through his hair. "I guess we'll have to go looking for them." He turned to Sandra. "Get in. I suspect they're just down the road."

Sandra quelled the nervous jumping of her stomach. Logan didn't seem worried. She was sure he had been through enough other things with the girls that this was simply another event.

But she couldn't stop her feelings of concern about the girls as she got into the van.

Logan lifted his hand to turn the key in the ignition. "Did I take the keys out?" he asked, turning to Sandra.

"Not that I remember," she replied.

He turned on a light on the dash that illuminated the interior of the van, then bent over to look. "Didn't drop them, either." He sat up, glancing sidelong at Sandra. "I suspect my dear little nieces took them."

"So what do we do?" she asked.

"We could wait."

"Or we could start walking," Sandra offered

quickly. The idea of sitting in the confines of the van felt too intimate to her.

"Okay. We walk," he agreed.

Logan got out and Sandra followed him, relief mingled with a tiny niggling of regret.

Chapter Eight

Logan clenched his fists at his sides, anger mixing with shame at what his nieces had done. They had gone too far this time.

"Can you figure which way they went?" Sandra asked.

"I'm guessing toward town." Logan bit down on his anger at the girls, hoping he was right. It could be a long night out here trying to find them if they decided they didn't want to be found. He stifled a flash of worry. Nothing had happened yet. He would find them.

Though Logan's eyes were accustomed to the dark, it was still slow walking down the road. Thankfully it was fairly wide, and the trees were more sparse at the top of the hill the road followed. Sandra was quiet, and Logan didn't know what to say.

Except to apologize for his nieces.

"I'm sorry about the girls," he said. "I keep hoping that one day they'll settle down and make some wise choices."

"It's okay, Logan. They're only ten, and I don't mind walking."

"Well, I do. I own a van. A nice van that works really well. I just hope they haven't lost the keys to it."

"I'm just glad they didn't try to start it. Brittany told me they used to drive their parents' van once in a while."

Logan snorted. "I'm not surprised. Linda and August let those girls do everything."

"Is that why you're so protective of them?"

Logan slipped his hands in his pockets as he walked along, considering his answer. "I've had to be. Their parents didn't always make the wisest choices."

"Do you mind telling me a little more about them?"

He hesitated.

"I think it would help me, if I'm going to be teaching them, to know what their family life was like," Sandra prompted.

"I suppose you're right," he conceded, glancing sidelong at her. She had gently probed before, when they were at Fort Walsh, and he had put her off. But now he knew she was as concerned about the girls as he was and as caught up in their schooling.

"My sister Linda used to flirt with every boy in sight," he said, searching for the right words, the right phrases. "Mostly it didn't matter because in a few months we would be moving to the next place my father wanted to go." He paused. His family's failings could still embarrass him, even in front of someone who lived almost the same lifestyle. "We were in one town longer than a few months, and my sister had been chasing a couple of boys around, playing one against the other. One was a good friend of mine, one of the few I ever got to know. He ended up in the hospital because the other guy beat him up. Linda thought it was funny. Worse than that, my mother thought it was a real honor that two guys would fight over her daughter. My dad, as usual, wasn't around.'' He shook his head, remembering the rage that flowed through him that day. His sister didn't seem to care. ''Then she got married. Had to, by the way. But things didn't change much. Commitment wasn't in her vocabulary. I know she left August at various times, hoping to find herself. Sometimes she took the girls, sometimes she didn't. My nieces grew up seeing that.''

''Did their parents love the girls?''

Logan blew out his breath as he considered Sandra's question. ''In their way, I suppose they did.''

''Then at least they had that.''

Logan glanced sidelong at her. He couldn't see her expression very clearly in the dark, but he detected a note of wistfulness in her voice.

''What was your childhood like?''

She had managed to find out things about him, but he still didn't know much of her.

She lifted her face to the dark sky as if looking for help there. ''This isn't part of my ongoing interview, is it?''

''No. But it is a way of making conversation while we're walking down this road,'' he said.

''A way of getting to know each other?''

Logan considered that. ''Partly.'' He wasn't sure how deeply he wanted to get involved in Sandra's life.

Yet on the other hand, she intrigued him. That and something deeper, more elemental. Something he had never experienced with a woman. "What was your father like?" he asked, fighting the direction of his thoughts.

Sandra wrapped her arms around herself as she seemed to consider her answer, as well.

They were so careful with each other, thought Logan. Each waiting, measuring, wondering how the other would judge them.

Sandra drew in a deep breath. "I guess the best way to describe my father is to call him the original guilt trip cruise guide. Even when I followed his lead and did what he wanted, I still felt as if I had completely disappointed him. Or my mother. So I did what any girl did who had spent most of her life trying to please a man who couldn't be pleased, and jumped ship."

Logan heard what she was saying and realized that while she had stated a basic conflict, she still hadn't told him much. "You do that often, don't you," he stated, glancing at her again.

"Do what?" She stopped, looking back.

Logan turned to face her, his hands still in his pockets. "Use words and figures of speech to give the idea that you're making conversation, that you're telling people something without really saying anything."

"Don't tell me you didn't understand what I was saying," she said, sounding slightly testy.

"I understood that he had expectations of you that differed from what you wanted. That's not so unusual. I understood that you didn't get along with your father. Neither did I. But you've really not told me anything."

Sandra sighed, looked away and then back again. "What do you want to know?"

Her eyes were two dark smudges, but as he stepped closer, he could see them glowing with a banked light. "I guess I'm only going to find out what you want to tell me, but I'd like to know more than that."

"Why?"

Her question hung between them, a whisper in the dark. He wasn't sure. Wasn't sure of the heightened feelings that resonated between them.

She was the complete opposite of everything he had ever wanted, but he couldn't stop the attraction he knew was growing between them. He wondered if she felt the same.

Then she turned and began walking, and he got his answer.

He caught up to her, but they said nothing more, the space between them greater than before.

Logan squinted through the dark, wondering how far the girls might have walked, wondering if they were okay. Hoping and praying that nothing had happened. The silence between him and Sandra was uncomfortable, and for the first time in a while, he missed the girls' chatter.

He heard Sandra cry out, and from the corner of his eye saw her stumble and fall heavily to the ground.

"Sandra, what happened?" He rushed to her side, dropping beside her. "Did you break something?"

"No, no," she gasped, clutching her knee. "I twisted my knee."

He didn't know first aid. Didn't know what to do. So he knelt beside her, helplessly watching as she pulled in one slow breath after another, her head pressed into the dirt as she moaned softly.

"What can I do? Let me help you."

She took in another labored breath and clenched her teeth. "Just wait. Just wait," she gasped.

Logan touched her shoulder, curved his hand around her to make some kind of connection, offer some kind of assistance.

Then she carefully lowered her leg.

"I think it's okay now," she said slowly. She tried to get up and would have fallen again. Logan caught her this time. Again she cried out, clutching his arm.

"Not so quick, Sandra," he said, holding her. "Take it easy."

"I need to get up. To keep moving." Her words were a thin thread of sound. Logan could tell she was in a lot of pain.

He slipped her arm around his neck and supported her as she struggled to her feet. Then, taking a few more slow breaths, she straightened.

"I'll be okay now," she said, pulling her arm back.

But Logan kept his other arm firmly clamped around her waist. "No, you won't."

She tried to take a step and faltered. Her breath hissed through clenched teeth.

"Take it easy, Sandra," he said quietly, holding her close to his side, supporting her easily.

"It's an old injury," she explained between breaths. "I tore ligaments last year."

Logan winced in sympathy. When he was a teen he'd strained ligaments, and he could vividly remember how much that hurt.

"I'll be okay," she added.

"No, you won't, and stop trying to be so tough," he reprimanded, his anger building. If the girls hadn't stolen the keys, this wouldn't have happened. Again he felt guilt and remorse over Sandra's pain.

"I think you should wait here while I try to find out where the girls are," Logan said, stopping.

Sandra looked at him, and in spite of the pain he knew she must be suffering, she managed a smile. "I think maybe I better stay with you. For the girls' sake."

In spite of his irritation, Logan managed to laugh.

"You're probably right," he said. "But this walking isn't going to be good for your knee."

"Truly, I need to keep moving a little bit, otherwise it will stiffen up on me."

Logan was surprised at how upbeat she sounded. She was tough, he had to give her that.

"Let me help you. We'll head to the van." He placed her arm across his shoulders again, holding on to her hand. To his surprise, she didn't object.

She took a step and leaned heavily on him as she took the next one.

Logan wanted to protest again, but he knew Sandra wasn't going to stop because he told her to. So he held her even closer.

He caught the scent of her hair. A faint night breeze teased strands of it, tickling his face in an altogether too pleasant way. Sandra didn't say anything, and Logan couldn't.

Their progress was slow, and periodically Logan would call out for the girls. Yet, as he held Sandra close to him, as his hand curved around her waist, he couldn't stop the insidious hope that he wouldn't find them quite yet.

"Where do you suppose the girls are?" Sandra asked, clinging to him.

Her voice sounded strained, as if she was fighting the pain. The tightening of his hand was an automatic, defensive gesture. To his surprise and pleasure, she didn't pull away.

"My guess would be they are either hiding a few minutes away from here or following us and too scared to show their faces," he said.

In the darkness her eyes glowed. She blinked and half turned. Logan shifted his weight. Then, instead of being side by side, they were face to face.

He held her eyes, felt his reason drifting away the longer they stayed facing each other, silent. It seemed the most normal thing, then, to lower his head.

Her faint protest brushed his lips, then faded as their mouths met and held.

A slow warmth spread through Logan as he held her closer, as he murmured her name against her lips. Her hands clung to his shoulders, her fingers pressing into him as she stood pliant in his arms.

Logan ignored the voice of reason that warned and chided. The voice that reminded him how little he really knew about Sandra. That reminded him of all the unknowns that swirled around her transient life.

But he couldn't keep the voices silent forever.

Reluctantly he pulled back. Lowered his hands.

Kissing her was a mistake, Logan told himself even as disappointment sifted through his rationalizations. Withdrawing was the right thing to do.

Logan repeated these words over and over again as Sandra turned and started hobbling away from him.

He caught up to her and was about to slip his arm around her again to support her.

"I don't need your help." Her voice sounded strained as she pushed his arm away.

Logan felt torn as he walked alongside her. Helping her had put him in this predicament. Yet he couldn't very well let her do worse damage to her knee.

"You shouldn't be walking," he said finally. "Why don't you sit down and wait while I try to find the girls."

Sandra didn't acknowledge his comment with words but moved to the side of the road and carefully lowered herself to the ground, still not looking at him.

Logan wished he could find the right words to ease the strain that had sprung up between them. Wished he could go back and erase the kiss they had shared.

Do you? Really?

His thoughts mocked him as he remembered the feel of her lips, the warmth of her arms. For a moment he had felt as if all was right with his world. As if all the frustrations of the past few months were but minor irritations that could be dealt with.

As long as he had Sandra.

Logan shook his head, as if to dislodge the enticement of those thoughts.

"Just stay here," he said gruffly. "I'll try to find the girls."

A rustle in the bushes ahead made him look up. In the darkness all he could see was two vague patches of white. They moved and then came slowly closer.

Bethany and Brittany.

"We're here, Uncle Logan," they said, voices subdued.

Logan clenched his fists at his side, took a deep breath and prayed for patience. He wanted to lash out at them for the pain they put Sandra through. For the situation they had created with their silly game.

"I think you had better give me the keys," he said quietly.

Brittany dug in the pockets of her shorts and pulled out a ring of keys. Their faint jangle was the only sound in the tense stillness that surrounded the four of them.

"You stay right here with Sandra. I'm going to get the van."

He knew they heard the suppressed anger in his voice because without a word they drifted to Sandra and sat beside her. They each took one of her hands. A silent plea for forgiveness. They glanced at Logan again.

Logan glared at them, knowing they couldn't make out his expression in the dark. But they felt his anger, because they quickly looked away.

He spun on his heel and marched up the hill, hoping his anger wouldn't make him fall and injure himself. That would just finish things off, he thought.

In a matter of minutes he was back in a swirl of dust that eddied in the headlights.

By the time he had his door open Sandra was standing, leaning on Brittany and Bethany as she hobbled to the van.

Logan opened the passenger door and held out his hand to help her in, but she ignored it.

The trip to Elkwater was made in absolute silence. A dozen comments ran through Logan's mind as he drove, but all of them sounded apologetic, which would be insincere, or encouraging, which would be wrong.

He got to Elkwater and slowed down.

"I should take you to the hospital," he said. "Get your knee looked at."

"No. It's not that bad," Sandra replied, her tone nonchalant.

"But you could have done some major damage to it. Especially if you've hurt it before."

Sandra shook her head, still not looking at him. "All the doctor is going to do is tell me that I have to stay off my foot and put a tensor bandage on it. I'm not going to go all the way into town just to find that out."

Logan couldn't help but glance behind him at his nieces. They were still looking suitably subdued, and he was sure they felt bad about what had happened to Sandra, as well.

He would deal with them later. Right now his main concern was for Sandra.

"I don't like this, Sandra. I don't think leaving it alone is such a good idea. It could get worse during the night, and then what?"

Sandra waved his comments away as they drove closer to her home. He still didn't like the idea of leaving her alone, but she was an adult and capable of making her own decisions.

He parked the van in front of her small home and was out and beside her van door before she could even get it open. In the dim glow of the streetlights, he could see the lines of pain etched on her features as she tried to get out on her own.

"Sandra, please. Don't be stubborn about this." He caught her by the shoulders and turned her to face him. "Let me take you to the hospital."

Sandra smiled. "Thanks for your concern, Logan. But truly, the only thing a doctor is going to do is poke around and twist it to see if I've torn anything, which really hurts. Then he's going to give me a prescription for painkillers, which I can't get filled until the next morning because there's no pharmacist on duty at two in the morning in a place the size of Medicine Hat."

What she said sounded reasonable. Yet Logan still felt the twist of guilt and the niggling feeling of wanting to do something to help her.

"You can walk me to the door, though, to make sure I don't fall again," she said.

Logan held out his arm, sensing that she wouldn't be comfortable with their previous arrangement. With another smile at him, she leaned on him as they walked. Logan couldn't stop himself from covering her arm, her skin soft under his hand. "Watch this step," he cautioned, leading her carefully around a large heave in the sidewalk.

Once again Logan found himself conscious of her beside him. Found himself pulling her a little closer than necessary. The fact that two pairs of eyes were watching them from the back of the van helped keep him from repeating the mistake he made on the hill a while ago.

"Where's your key?" he asked as they made it up the front step of her house.

"It's not locked," she said, reaching over and opening the door.

"That's not a good idea, Sandra. This is the best way to get robbed."

He felt Sandra's shrug, her way of dismissing his concern, as they stepped into the darkened house. "I don't have much worth stealing," she said, fumbling for the switch just inside the door.

The room was lit by the jewellike glow of the stained glass lamps. "I don't know about that," Logan said, his eyes caught by their soothing glow. "Those lamps must be worth a lot."

"Maybe," Sandra said. "But not too many people are buying them. A thief might have a hard time fencing them." She let go of his arm as she lowered herself onto the couch, carefully lifting her knee.

Logan bit his lip, loath to leave her. "How do you figure on getting to bed?"

"I just might stay here for the night. I can keep my leg elevated that way."

"Do you have any ice I can put on it? I'm sure that would help if there's any swelling."

Sandra shook her head as she lay back on the couch. "No. I'm fine, Logan. You should get those girls to bed."

Still he couldn't leave, guilt and an indefinable emotion he didn't want to explore keeping him beside her.

"Do you have anything I can get you for the pain?"

Sandra smiled at him. But it was a gentle smile, warm and friendly. Logan felt the curl of attraction and had to stop himself from moving toward her. He dismissed his feelings as the natural protectiveness of a man with a defenseless woman.

A defenseless, wholly appealing woman, he amended, his eyes following the curve of her smile, the dark spill of her hair over her shoulder.

Go now, he told himself. *She doesn't need or want anything from you right now.*

But still he lingered.

"Don't worry about working tomorrow. Me and the girls will figure something out." He slipped his hands into his back pockets, rocking on his heels. "I feel so bad about what happened."

"It was just an accident, Logan." Sandra raised herself on one elbow. "And please, don't come down too hard on the girls. They're young. What they did was wrong, I know, but I don't think they knew precisely what they were doing." Her dark eyes were full of concern.

Logan bit back a harsh reply, disagreeing with her. The girls knew exactly what they were doing, only the consequences had been greater than they realized. But he sensed, in Sandra's plea on behalf of Brittany and Bethany, something more than a simple defense of their actions.

"Please, Logan?" she repeated.

"I'm not going to beat them and lock them in their rooms with a ration of bread and water, if that's what you're worried about," Logan assured her. "I know they feel pretty bad about what happened. But I do have to make them see that there are consequences to their actions. Make them see that they have to think about that before they do something even more foolish."

Sandra nodded and leaned back, her brow smooth as if what he said had reassured her. "You're a good uncle to them, Logan. I hope they appreciate it."

Her unexpected compliment softened the defense he had been building against her ever since that misguided kiss in the hills. He found that he couldn't look away. Didn't want to look away.

Her expression grew serious. He saw the faint lift of her throat as she swallowed.

Then she turned her head and closed her eyes. "You better go, Logan."

He went to the door, knowing she was right. Yet just before he closed the door behind himself, he couldn't stop from looking at her one more time.

But her eyes were still closed, and as Logan shut the door behind him, he wondered what she was thinking.

Chapter Nine

Sandra listened to Logan's steps as he walked down the sidewalk. Then the sound of a door closing, an engine starting.

Sandra blew out her breath forcing away the memories of Logan holding her, the concern in his voice, the touch of his mouth on hers...

"Stop right there," she said aloud. "Get ready for bed."

The hot flashes of pain centered on her injured knee pushed everything else out of her mind. She slowly lowered her leg, pushed herself up and caught her balance. It took her a few minutes to get to the bathroom, to down the last two painkillers she had and find the tensor bandage to wrap around her knee.

Her movements were awkward and fraught with pain as she got into bed. She turned off the small bedside lamp and settled back, waiting for the painkillers to take effect.

Fifteen minutes later, she painfully rolled onto her

side. Instead of sleep bringing its blessed memory loss, it was as if the loneliness of the dark pressed in on her. A loneliness made all the sharper because of what she had shared just an hour ago with Logan.

Don't go there, she warned herself. Going back to that moment was a mistake. For both of them.

So why did it feel so wrong to dismiss him? He wasn't the man she had been looking for all her life. In fact, Logan was the exact opposite of what she wanted.

But what do you want? she asked herself. *Someone like Henri who lives free and easy then stiffs you? Do you enjoy living hand to mouth, spending more time avoiding what you don't want instead of figuring out what you do?*

Her words accused her, underscoring the dissatisfaction that grew with each wrong decision, each stumbling mistake she made in her life. She had left her home, her father and his unceasing expectations, hoping to find an elusive peace.

Peace I leave with you; My Peace I give you. I do not give to you as the world gives. Do not let your hearts be troubled and do not be afraid.

The words that drifted through her mind were familiar, safe. Words from her past. Words she had heard and read many times. She wasn't exactly sure where in the Bible they were found, she only knew they were words of comfort.

So what did they mean to her?

Sandra rolled carefully onto her back again, wincing at the pain in her knee. Unbidden came memories of other times she was in bed, hurting or sick. Her mother's hand on her forehead. A cup of juice or soda on the bedside table.

The gentle weight of her mother's body as she would sit on the mattress, lightly stroking Sandra's head.

Sandra stifled a cry at the memory. Her mother had been Sandra's defense, her refuge. But she was gone. Sandra pressed her hand against her mouth as she looked around the room. How had she come here, to a rented place and short of money?

Running away. Leaving the heaviness of expectations she could never meet. Leaving the constant disapproval of a father who always wanted more than she could give.

Honor your father and your mother, so that you may live long in the land the Lord your God is giving you.

She had tried, Sandra thought, remembering the commandment laid out in Exodus. She had tried to live up to their expectations until she knew she would crumple under the weight of those expectations unless she could flee and find herself.

Memories of her parents began to intermingle with thoughts of Logan. She wondered why he had kissed her. Sandra knew what Logan thought of her. He disapproved of her lifestyle, of her choices. Not that she should care. He wasn't her type.

Then why did she feel so right in his arms? Why had she felt safe with him?

Sandra closed her eyes as her thoughts became muzzy. With a light sigh, she released all her concerns and let her mind wander.

But her last thoughts were of Logan.

His arms around her, holding her close.

Peace.

* * *

"I'm going to go to Sandra's now," Logan said, standing over his nieces. They sat at the dining room table, papers scattered around, their heads bent, looking properly contrite. "I'll be back in about twenty minutes and I'll expect that you'll have those problems Sandra gave you done by then."

He had taken them into town early this morning to pick up a pair of crutches, but as soon as they came home, he put them to work.

Brittany glanced at him, then her eyes flicked away. In that brief look Logan saw sorrow and regret. Logan felt a flutter of sympathy for them. What they had done was silly, but if Sandra hadn't hurt herself, their actions would only have been a nuisance. And what did they know of responsibility. They were only ten. Most of their lives had been spent with parents who would merely laugh at what had happened last night.

Logan steeled himself against those thoughts. The girls had to learn consequences, and feeling sorry for what happened in the past was only part of it.

"Is Sandra going to come and teach us today?" Bethany asked in a small voice.

"It all depends on her," Logan said. "She might be able to walk using these crutches."

Brittany set her pencil down, folded her hands demurely on her lap. "Are we going back to Calgary after you see Sandra?"

"I don't know, Brittany." He had thought of it. But he still hadn't come up with a plan for the Jonserad home he was satisfied with. He had phoned Ian, his partner, who didn't sound too eager for Logan to come back. He suspected that had more to do with Ian angling for a long vacation once Logan was back.

He wasn't going to tell the girls this. Better they didn't know. And it would also be better if they didn't know what had happened last night between him and Sandra.

The memory teased him, dancing on the edge of his consciousness. He had tried to forget it, but in every weak moment images of Sandra returned.

It was a momentary lapse, he reminded himself, pulling his thoughts to the present.

"Are you going to stay at Sandra's for a while?" Brittany asked, her expression guileless.

But Logan knew better and sensed more than heard the hopefulness in her voice.

"I'm going to bring the crutches to her and then I'm coming straight back." He held Brittany's eye and decided to bring things out in the open. "And I know what you girls were doing last night and what you've been trying to do ever since you met Sandra."

Brittany blinked as her mouth drooped. "What were we doing?" she asked, a false innocencecoating her words.

"Brittany, I may be older than you but I'm not dumb. I've seen the movies you've seen, too. I know all about young girls who think they can play matchmaker for their unsuspecting uncles or fathers or brothers or whatever hapless male ends up in their life. That's what you girls were doing last night."

Brittany's eyes grew wide as her shoulders slumped in defeat. "No, Uncle Logan. We weren't trying to do that at all." She tossed her sister a look of panic-stricken appeal. "Were we, Bethany?"

But of the two of them, poor Bethany was blessed with an overabundance of conscience, and she couldn't look her uncle in the face. She concentrated fiercely on her work, her pencil making dark marks on the paper.

"Don't try it again," Logan warned, his hands resting on his hips as he stared Brittany down. "I'm sure Sandra is a wonderful person, but she just isn't my type. We're leaving here, she's leaving here, and we'll probably never see her again."

Brittany blinked, licked her lips and looked down, defeated.

Logan waited a beat, as if to press the point home, then he turned and left.

But as he walked toward Sandra's house, he couldn't help but think that his stern words were directed as much to himself as to the girls.

He'd tried all morning to pass off the protective feeling he had toward Sandra. How she'd felt in his arms.

Get a grip, he reminded himself. He was acting as silly as any of the young boys he saw on the beach every day, flirting with the girls they met, feeling safe in the transitory nature of summer flings.

As he had told Bethany and Brittany, the reality was he was going back to Calgary, and Sandra was...

He wasn't sure what Sandra was going to do, and he suspected she didn't know, either.

Sandra was sitting outside in a dilapidated beach chair when he came up the winding street to her house. He should have phoned, he thought. Should have warned her he was coming.

But as he watched her, he was glad he caught her unawares.

She lay with her head back, a smile teasing her lips. Her hair hung loose, lustrous in the bright sun. One leg was up on a chair, a tensor bandage white against her skin. She wore shorts and a loose top that set off her tanned skin and dark hair.

Logan's steps slowed as he watched her, a part of him captivated by her beauty, his more practical part taking in the strings hanging from the side of the lawn chair, her faded and worn shorts. She was a woman who rejected all the things important to him. Stability. Home. Family.

He pushed those thoughts aside. He didn't want to think about that. Didn't want to think about anything, really. For a brief moment, he was tired of being responsible and making sensible decisions. For a moment, he envied Sandra's relative freedom.

"Hey there," he said, forcing a light tone to his voice as he came nearer.

Her head jerked up, her eyes met his, and time became nothing.

The reality of their kiss from last night hovered between them, as real as the breeze that fanned their cheeks. Logan couldn't help but look at her mouth, wondering if she was thinking of it, as well.

"Hey, yourself," she said finally, breaking the contact. She bent her head over her bandage, fussing unnecessarily with it. "I'm sorry I couldn't come this morning."

"I didn't expect you to." He walked to her side and set the crutches beside her chair. "I brought you these.

Since you wouldn't go to the doctor, I figured we could at least follow his advice."

As Sandra looked up, her smile spread, transforming her face. "So you've appointed yourself my doctor as well as my conscience."

Logan shrugged her comment aside and glanced around. He found a plastic lawn chair nearby and pulled it closer. Ignoring the dust on the seat, he sat down.

"How did you sleep last night?" he asked, leaning forward, his elbows resting on his knees, hoping he sounded more restrained than he felt.

She waggled her hand in front of him. "So-so. I kept waking up when I had to roll over. But the knee is already much better."

"Are you sure you don't want to see a doctor?"

Sandra laughed, pushing her hair from her face in a casually graceful gesture. "I'm sure. It would be a waste of time." She glanced at the crutches. "So don't tell me that you come equipped to cover all contingencies?"

"I went into town this morning with the girls to pick them up for you."

Sandra tilted her head slightly, as if studying him from another angle. "You what?"

"You heard me."

She quirked her lips in a half smile, tucking her hair behind her ear. "I did, but I can't believe you went through all that trouble for me."

"The girls figured the sooner you were mobile, the sooner you could come back to teach them." As soon as he said the words, he realized how they sounded.

Brittany and Bethany had nothing to do with him getting her crutches.

Her smile slipped, and Logan knew that she understood the implication, as well. "I see." That was all she said. Then she lowered her leg and reached down to pick the crutches up. "Well, I guess the sooner I get used to these things, the quicker I can go back to work."

"There's no rush, Sandra," he said quietly, still feeling guilty, wishing she would smile at him again. "I wasn't trying to tell you that you have to come back right away."

Sandra didn't reply. She stood, fitted the crutches under her arms and made her way down the sidewalk and back again. Logan stood, ready to catch her if she fell, almost hoping he could come swooping to her rescue again. But she made it on her own, handling the crutches with confidence.

"They work and they fit good." She glanced at him, then away. "I guess there's no reason I should stay moping around here, is there? We can leave right away."

Logan felt a twinge of disappointment. He wasn't quite ready to go back to the twins and share Sandra with them. In spite of his previous self-castigation, he would have liked to spend a few moments with her. Just the two of them.

He wasn't sure what he wanted from her. He only knew that no matter how he scolded and reminded himself of her unsuitability, being with her only a few moments brushed all those objections away as easily as cobwebs.

"I have a few notes I wrote down from last night," Sandra said, shaking her hair and glancing at him. "Would you mind getting them for me? They're on the low table in the living room."

"Gladly done," he said.

Logan stepped inside her home, unable to keep from looking around. The house looked as shabby as it had before. The furniture was poor, though he knew none of it belonged to either Sandra or her roommate.

He sighed, knowing he shouldn't judge Sandra by her lack of possessions, but her house reminded him clearly of his upbringing. How his parents had so often decried material possessions and said they didn't matter. In his walk with God he had discovered that his parents were right, but somehow they had forgotten the responsibility they had to their children to at least provide them with some of the basics.

Logan thrust the memories aside even as he was thankful for the equilibrium they gave him. The reminder of how empty other life choices can be.

The papers Sandra wanted lay in a neat pile on the table. As he bent to pick them up, he absently glanced at the pad of paper beside them.

"Dear Dad, I hope you are well. I need..." That was all that was written across the top of the pad in flowing handwriting as delicate as lace. "I need..." what? Money? Help?

Logan felt a flush of guilt, knowing he shouldn't have read it. Brief and unfinished the note may be, but the words were meant for someone else. Did she write her father often requesting help? How convenient for her, he thought with a flush of anger.

He turned away. It was none of his business. Sandra had never told him much about her father and he doubted she ever would. Their lives weren't that intertwined.

Sandra was waiting outside. "Good. You found them." She flashed him a bright smile. In spite of what he had remembered in her house, he couldn't stop his reaction to her. Angry with himself, he looked away.

"I'll carry these for you," he said.

"Thanks. I appreciate it." She didn't seem to notice anything as she started toward his cabin. Logan slowed his steps to match hers.

"So what nefarious punishment did you dream up for the girls?" she asked.

"They wanted to come with me to bring the crutches, but I wouldn't let them. I'm hoping you will put them through their paces."

"Thanks. I get to be the heavy."

Logan wanted to be able to come back with a witty reply, but then he made the mistake of looking at her. A mischievous smile lit her mouth, her eyes seemed to twinkle, and memories of their last time together slipped into his mind. As he held Sandra's animated gaze, he wondered if she was thinking about last night, as well.

Several times he wanted to bring up what happened, but he didn't know how to broach the subject. Didn't know if it was something he should apologize for or if he should simply act as if kissing his nieces' tutor was a casual way of saying thanks.

"Sandra, I want to talk about—"

"No, you don't," she interrupted him. She quickened her pace, the rubber tips of the crutches making soft clumping sounds on the sidewalk. "And neither do I." She sounded defensive, almost angry.

She *was* thinking about last night, he realized.

So he said nothing. She said nothing. And the rest of the trip to his cabin was made in a reproving silence.

The girls welcomed Sandra with cries of apology and a few tears. Sandra forgave them, and in a matter of minutes they were all seated at the table in the main living area. Logan waited a moment, watching, then he retreated to his room, hoping and praying inspiration and forgetfulness would come to him.

Four hours and six cups of coffee later, he had managed to come up with a reasonable design. Not exceptional, but he was realizing that exceptional was beyond his capabilities. A depressing thought.

He pushed himself away from his drafting table and stretched to work the kinks out of his back. All day, he had had a hard time concentrating on what he was doing. Part of his attention had been on his work, but most had been on the subdued chatter coming from the other part of the cabin. Sandra's deep voice, counterpointed by the hushed sounds of the girls, seemed designed to create a minimum of annoyance.

He got up, and the moment he entered the living room, three pairs of eyes shot to his.

He felt like a dictator surveying the troops. "At ease," he joked, coming to stand beside Bethany. "How's it going?"

"Good, Uncle Logan," she said with forced brightness, her gaze going to the book in front of her.

Logan glanced at Brittany, who averted her eyes,

then at Sandra. But she didn't look away. Her head was angled in a purely defensive gesture, and he didn't like it.

"I'm going to get supper going," he said, striving for a nonchalant tone to break the tension that held everyone in thrall. "Would you like to stay, Sandra?"

"Yes, please stay for supper," Brittany said.

"You can't cook for yourself with your leg so sore," Bethany added.

Sandra smiled at the girls, but Logan could see her wavering. *Probably thinks I'm going to attack her again,* he thought.

"I think the girls are right," he said quietly, adding his voice to theirs. "And if they help me, it will be their way of letting you know how sorry they are."

He caught Bethany's aggrieved look, but a quick frown from him erased it from her face. "Good idea, Uncle Logan," she said meekly.

Sandra's gaze skittered over his face, then away. "Okay. I won't say no to a meal I don't have to cook."

"Great. Are the girls done?" Logan asked.

"Brittany can go. Bethany just needs a few minutes to finish up what she's doing."

Logan nodded to Brittany, who still looked far from pleased. They'd have to have a little talk while peeling potatoes, he realized.

Sandra bit her lip as she watched Logan walk out of the room, Brittany trailing behind him. She should have refused supper, she thought. Especially after what happened last night.

It still hung between them, that stolen kiss. She

didn't know why it should have had such an impact on her, but it had. For a moment she had had this utter feeling of rightness.

Of peace.

Then, on the way here, she knew Logan wanted to talk about it. To dissect it.

To apologize and erase it.

She didn't want him to and had cut him off. It might have been better for both of them if they had simply discussed it as mature adults.

She looked around the cozy cabin and sighed. She shouldn't stay. No matter how nonchalant she wanted to be about Logan, undercurrents swirled around them each time they were together. She wasn't sure of her footing anymore, of where she wanted to be.

But the thought of going to her empty cabin to sit with her leg up didn't measure up to the dangerous appeal of being with Logan in a more relaxed setting.

She was playing a dire game, she warned herself as she gathered Brittany's work. And worst of all, she knew it.

It was just that she was so tired of being alone. The past week had been more enjoyable than she had imagined. Working with the girls and seeing their faces light up when they understood something she had been trying to tell them was more fulfilling than anything she had done since graduating from school.

How ironic that she ended up enjoying the very thing she had been running away from.

"I'm done, Sandra." Bethany closed her book, and Sandra's attention was drawn sharply to the young girl.

"Good. You can go and help your uncle."

Bethany nodded and slipped out of her chair.

Sandra finished cleaning up the papers and books, listening all the while to the sounds coming from the kitchen. The low rumble of Logan's voice patiently explaining what had to be done. The clank of pots on the stove, water running. A question from one of the girls. Logan explaining again.

Sandra felt a sharp pang as she listened. The only time her father had ever been in the kitchen was to get a glass of water from the fridge. She couldn't imagine her father doing what Logan was doing right now.

She didn't want to compare Logan to her father, but she couldn't help it. Every man she had met in the past five years had been measured against Josh Bachman. The closer they were to him, the quicker she ran in the other direction.

So she ended up with someone like Henri, who was about as far removed from her father in temperament as a cocker spaniel was from a Doberman. But thanks to Henri and his scheming, she was stuck in this town, trying to find a way out of the economic hole she had dug for herself.

But she didn't want to think about that now.

Tomorrow will worry about itself. Each day has enough trouble of its own.

The familiar words drifted into Sandra's consciousness. She knew they were from the Bible. Her mother used to quote them time and time again.

She stacked books neatly in a pile and carefully maneuvered her leg around the table to get to her feet. The crutches were definitely a help, she thought as she worked her way to the kitchen. Once again, she was thankful that Logan had gone through the trouble to get them for her. Of course, as he said, it was only because of the girls, but she still appreciated it.

"Do you need any help?" she asked, pausing in the doorway.

Logan glanced over his shoulder, smiling at her.

"No. I think we can manage."

Sandra felt the all too familiar jump of her stomach at the sight of his smile. "I'm feeling a little guilty sitting in that room without doing anything," she added.

"Well, we're a little cramped in here right now, but you can keep us company. Sit yourself down by the table if you want." Logan angled his chin toward the dining nook.

Sandra worked her way around the counter where the girls were chopping up the fixings for a salad. They glanced quickly at her. Each flashed her a smile and then went back to work.

Sandra was amazed at how reserved they were. In fact all afternoon they had been very cooperative and quiet. Not at all their usual selves. Sandra wondered what Logan had told them to create such meekness.

She carefully lowered herself in the chair, laying the crutches on the floor beside her. As she looked up she caught Brittany's cheeky grin. Her careful wink.

And she realized that the girls may be down but not out.

She glanced at Logan again and for a moment felt sorry for him and the responsibility of these two rambunctious young girls.

At that moment he chanced a look her way.

It was just a casual turning of his head, a quick glance. He was stirring a pot.

But as their eyes met, his hands slowed, she swallowed, and it was as if everything around them slipped away. As if there were only the two of them, and nothing else mattered.

Chapter Ten

"Now it will be easier to make a circle when we pray," Brittany said brightly, holding out her hand to Sandra.

Logan set the pan of spaghetti carefully on the table then sat down between Bethany and Sandra. He tossed Brittany a warning glance, but she had already bowed her head. Bethany had his hand, and he had no choice but to hold out his other hand for Sandra.

Without looking up, she laid hers in his. Her fingers were cool and soft, and as Logan closed his hand over hers, he felt the tiny ridge of a scar.

He couldn't stop the faint tremor of his heart at the fragility of her hand in his.

Then he, too, bent his head to pray, forcing thoughts of Sandra aside as he asked God for a blessing on the food. He prayed for his mother, for the girls. After a heartbeat of silence, he prayed for Sandra. Silently, he prayed that he could keep his senses around her, but out loud he prayed that she would be kept in God's care and that her knee would heal.

As soon as he said amen Sandra slid her hand out of his. The girls began chattering, asking Sandra what kind of dressing she wanted on her salad, how much pasta.

They were attentive and gracious hostesses, and Logan was pleased with their behavior.

But all through supper, Sandra avoided his gaze. As if that moment just before supper was ready hadn't happened.

But Logan didn't have to speak. The girls filled in all the dead air with their chattering. Logan didn't know how, after spending most of their days with Sandra, they could have much more to say to each other, but they managed.

After being prompted by the girls, Logan obediently told Sandra about the condo they lived in.

"It's right on the Bow River and has a huge balcony," Bethany added.

"And Uncle Logan said if he gets the Jonserad project, then we might be able to buy a house with a yard." Brittany looked at Logan as if for confirmation.

He nodded, realizing that for the moment he was superfluous.

"What is the Jonserad project?" Sandra asked, her gaze glancing off Logan's.

"It's a home I'm designing for an older couple."

"He's got some really good ideas," Brittany said, scraping the last of the spaghetti off her plate. "Can I show her, Uncle Logan?"

"No. I don't think that's necessary. I'm sure Sandra

isn't interested." Logan gave Brittany his I'm serious look, and thankfully she backed off.

"You know that Uncle Logan doesn't like anyone to see what he's working on," Bethany added, chiding her sister.

Logan caught Brittany discreetly giving Bethany a reproving poke and chose to ignore it. He couldn't be refereeing them all the time. And sometimes he couldn't blame either of them. Bethany had a tendency toward self-righteousness, which often antagonized Brittany's fractious side.

"Are you done, Brittany?" he asked, holding her gaze.

She nodded.

"Then you and Bethany can clear up the dishes and wash up."

"If we do that, can we get some ice cream for dessert?"

"I don't think it would be a good idea for Sandra to try to walk on the beach with crutches," Logan said, glancing at Sandra.

"You could stay here with her and we could get it." Brittany made the offer brightly.

Logan stifled a sigh, knowing exactly where Brittany was going with this. In spite of his warnings, the girls just didn't give up. But he had to confess that he didn't mind the idea of being alone with Sandra again, either.

"Okay. But first the dishes."

The girls moved faster than Logan had ever seen. In a manner of minutes and without any arguments whatsoever, they had the table cleared, the dishes done and the counters wiped as clean as a surgeon's table.

Brittany hung up the dish towel while Bethany sidled up to Logan and leaned against him. Logan smiled and slipped his arm around her waist. Her head came just past his shoulder. He turned to look at her, and for a moment he wondered how long it would be before she stopped these spontaneous shows of affection.

"Can I have the money for ice cream, Uncle Logan?"

"I should have known better," Logan said, tickling Bethany. She pulled back, giggling. "Here I thought you were being all sweet and nice because I'm such a great guy."

"You are," Bethany said, still laughing. "But we don't have any money for the ice cream. And you do."

Logan hitched himself sideways, pulling his wallet out of his pants pocket. He slipped a few bills in Bethany's hand and winked at her. "I want a chocolate swirl, dipped with sprinkles," he said. Then he turned to Sandra. "And what about you?"

"Just vanilla is fine," she said with a smile in Bethany's direction.

"I expect to get the change back," Logan called as Bethany spun around and the girls bolted from the room.

"You will, Uncle Logan." Brittany's words drifted back and were cut off by the dull slam of the wooden screen door.

It was as if the entire house had deflated.

Logan turned to Sandra, smiling, as he sat across from her. "Amazing how quiet it gets when they're gone."

Sandra wasn't looking at him. Instead she was toying

with a flower petal that had fallen from the wildflower arrangement in the center of the table. "They sure listen well to you," she said quietly.

Logan searched her features, wondering if her words commended or condemned.

"At times they do," he replied, watching as she carefully unfolded the small blue petal, her movements unhurried. He wanted to find out more about her even as he questioned the wisdom of it. They were going to be parting ways, and when they did, it would be to their own separate lives. Better if he kept things superficial.

"Do you want to sit outside while we wait for the girls?" he asked. "It's so nice this time of the evening."

"Sure." She gave him a polite smile and pushed her chair back. Logan handed her the crutches, helping her to her feet.

Once again they were facing each other, Logan's hand on her arm. Once again Logan felt awareness arcing between them, real and tangible.

But this time reason ruled, and he took a quick step back from her.

Sandra led the way, and Logan followed. Once on the deck, Logan made sure she had an extra chair for her leg. He sat down, stretching his legs out in front of him.

In spite of the undercurrents that had flowed between them a few moments ago, he felt a curious peace drifting over him.

It had been a long while since he'd had a woman

over for supper. It had been entirely pleasant to see the girls interact with Sandra. In spite of their constant maneuvering to get him and Sandra together, Brittany and Bethany didn't seem as calculating around Sandra as they did with Karen. With Sandra it was as if they had found someone they could connect with, someone they were comfortable around.

"I'm surprised you let the girls go get ice cream."

Logan glanced sidelong at Sandra, aware that he had been quiet for a while.

"I thought you would have had them locked in their bedrooms with bread and water," Sandra continued, her eyes flicking to his then away.

Logan had to laugh. "I'm not very creative when it comes to thinking up punishments. They did have to work pretty hard on their math once we were back from town, but I couldn't think of anything else. They feel pretty bad about what happened."

Sandra nodded, acknowledging his comment, and the conversation lagged. He wondered how to say what he really wanted to. They were alone, and it would probably be their last chance until he and the girls left for Calgary. He wanted to clear up what happened last night. Wanted to let her know that he wasn't in the habit of kissing just any woman.

And what had it meant to you? He rubbed his forehead as he glanced sidelong at Sandra.

She was staring straight ahead, twirling a strand of hair around her finger.

He didn't know what to say to her.

"What school will the girls be attending in the fall?" Sandra asked finally.

"McIntyre Elementary."

Sandra nodded, giving her hair another twist. "I imagine you'll be looking for another tutor once you go back to Calgary?" Her tone was perfectly reasonable, businesslike almost, which made her comment seem even more stark.

"I've got my secretary in Calgary still looking for me." He couldn't imagine that she would have much more success finding anyone now than she had before Logan had been forced to ask Sandra.

"And if you don't find someone?"

Logan bit back a sigh. "I don't want to think about that." He didn't. Because if he did, he knew he would be asking Sandra if she would be willing to come and tutor the girls.

And he knew, in spite of his attraction toward her, that would be a mistake. It was as if he had to remind himself again and again of his responsibility to his nieces. What they did last night showed him more clearly than ever the need for stability in their lives. If Sandra did come to Calgary, how long would she stay, given her employment record?

"And what are your plans once we leave here?" he asked, almost afraid of her answer.

"I have that lamp order to work on, and from there—" she shrugged "—I'll have to see where the wind blows me." She released the strand of hair she'd been playing with.

Logan felt a stab of disappointment. He should have known that.

He thought of the letter she'd started to her father.

"Do you see your father often on your meanderings around the country?"

Sandra stiffened, then lowered her hand to her lap. "I keep in touch with him."

Dear Dad, I need... The beginning of her letter came back to him. "Have you seen him lately?"

Sandra's gaze flicked to him. She seemed curious and defensive at the same time. "I haven't seen him for five years. When I told him I wasn't going to teach, he told me to leave. Told me not to bother coming back until I had a real job. I don't think what I'm doing now would constitute a real job."

Beneath the cool delivery of her words, Logan couldn't help but catch a note of pain.

"Do you miss him?"

Sandra threw him an angry look, but then like a deflating balloon, she sank back in her chair. "My dad and I were never close," she said abruptly. "My mother and I did more together than he did."

"And where is your mother?"

Sandra looked away, then at her hands twined in her lap. "My mother died when I was in my third year of college."

Logan felt himself grow absolutely still. He had always assumed that her mother was still alive.

He watched her nervous movements, felt a wave of pity well up in him.

He said nothing, sensing that more would come if he waited.

Listened.

"They haven't kissed yet." Brittany pulled behind the corner of the empty cabin beside Uncle Logan's.

She looked at Bethany. "What are we going to do?"

Bethany bit her lip. "We can wait a few more minutes but we have to get the ice cream soon or Uncle Logan is going to think we're scheming again."

Brittany sighed and looked at her most uncooperative uncle. "At least they kissed each other once already."

Bethany giggled at the memory. "And we prayed together tonight. That's a good thing."

Brittany nodded. "Well, we can't wait too much longer. We should go."

Sandra sat back in her chair, looking past the cabins to the lake beyond.

It had been a long time since anyone had asked her about her family, and even then it was just in passing. Cora usually was discussing how to make her next fortune and flitted in and out of Sandra's life like a moth.

Now, after knowing her only a few weeks, Logan was asking her about her mother.

Sandra drew in a slow breath as memories of her mother, like pages of a photo album, flipped through her mind.

"My mother was always my last line of defense," she said softly, breaking the long silence.

"What do you mean?"

Sandra chanced a glance at Logan, wondering what he would think, wondering if he would really understand. Suddenly, she wanted him to. Wanted him to be able to see what her youth had been like.

"My dad had high expectations of me. My mother

did, too, but she was more realistic. With my father it was as if all the plans he'd had for four children were put on the one he did have. Me.'' Sandra ran her finger up and down the arm of her chair. "He'd go over my homework every night with me, and if it wasn't right, I'd have to do it again. My social life was well guarded, as well. Only certain friends, and they all had to come from church.''

She stopped, remembering the confrontations and the struggles.

"You said your mother was your defense,'' Logan said quietly.

Sandra nodded, smiling. "My mother was more pragmatic. She'd invite over a few of the neighborhood kids once in a while. When Dad was gone at conferences, she'd rent frivolous videos. She tried to create a balance when she could, but my father was very domineering. As I got older she knew they hadn't raised a genius, so she could usually get my father to tone his expectations down. By grade nine, when he realized I wasn't going to be a physicist or an engineer, he was willing to settle for mere professor. My mother talked him into letting me become a teacher.'' She laughed, but it wasn't a happy sound.

"Did you want to?''

Sandra shrugged. "I never had a chance to figure out what I wanted. My dad told me, and when I was younger I listened. Then I became a teenager, and everything changed.''

She stopped, staring straight ahead at nothing, her mind's eye going back to the many confrontations they had over her clothes, her friends, her studies. Anything and everything.

"But you finished your degree."

"I was programmed to." She tried for lighthearted but missed the mark. "Finish what you start," she continued. "So I did. After Mom died, Dad started pushing again. Started pulling strings to make sure that I got just the right kind of job in just the right kind of school." Sandra closed her eyes, rubbing her forehead with one finger as if erasing a memory. "The daughter of Josh Bachman wasn't going to get just any old job. I wanted to do things on my own, but he wouldn't hear of it. I was going to quit, but thank goodness a friend talked me into staying. Told me that I might never know when my education would come in handy. She was right." She angled her head to look at him. "Because here I am."

Logan sat back slowly, as if absorbing this new information. "And when you left, you stopped going to church."

Sandra's mouth lifted in a faint smile, and she slanted Logan a quick sidewise glance. "You don't give up on that, do you?"

"I guess it's because God doesn't give up on you, either."

Things were getting heavy, Sandra thought. She remembered the evening in her cabin. After Logan and the girls had left. The compelling music. The faint touch of God's hand.

Sandra tilted her head, forcing herself to make a light comment. "I suppose this is where you are going to tell me that if I go to the church of my choice, I will find the God Who doesn't give up on me.''

Logan moved in his chair, pulling it closer. Sandra found she didn't mind. Didn't mind his concern or the fact that he so easily spoke of things she hadn't discussed with anyone in a long time. "Church is one place to find God," he said quietly.

"Nature is another," she countered. "And I like the God I find in nature much better."

"Same God."

"Not the way I've seen it. Church is stifling and restrictive. I mean, look at the whole idea. Ten commandments read each Sunday. All a bunch of don'ts." She spoke the words with a little more force than necessary. As if she was trying to convince herself, she thought.

"The freedom of discipline."

"Pardon me?"

Logan smiled lightly, a dimple winking at her from one corner of his mouth. "There's freedom in rules."

"Okay, that begs an explanation." Sandra adjusted her leg on the chair ahead of her, wondering what Logan meant. "And I think you can give me one."

Logan shrugged, looked down as if gathering his thoughts. "Freedom isn't always as freeing as you think. I can do what I do because I had the discipline to stick with what I was doing. I didn't learn that from my parents."

"I did," she said softly. "Nothing so wonderful about it."

"Are you doing what you want?"

Logan's question wound itself around her heart,

slowly pulling up her self-doubts, her moments when she understood that her freedom hadn't been exactly freeing. "I thought I was," she said quietly. "I really thought I was."

"So what happened?"

"I think I lost my way," Sandra said, fiddling with the material of her skirt, unable to meet his eyes. "I was the one with all the chances, all the support, and here I am, floundering. You who had to figure it out yourself, you know what you want."

"It's in how you start, Sandra. You started with a no. No to God, no to your family. That doesn't take you far. Doesn't take you anywhere, if you don't know what you are going to say yes to. God says yes to us. Our life with Him isn't just a list of do nots. It's freedom within discipline. I am where I am because I said yes to God's yes. I knew what I wanted better than what I didn't want."

Sandra felt a deep sadness overwhelm her. She didn't want to examine her life anymore. "I told you about my parents," she said, forcing herself to sound bright, cheery, carefree. "Tell me more about yours."

Logan held her gaze, his hazel eyes steady on hers. "My parents raised Linda and myself to be free. We were allowed to do what we wanted. But it went both ways, because so were my parents. Like I said, there were times we didn't have enough to eat because my parents were exercising their own freedom. Which, in turn, restricted what Linda and I could do. I only started feeling truly free when I went to school. When I disciplined myself to learn something." He looked at Sandra, holding her gaze, his expression serious.

"When I gave my life to God and let Him make the decisions in my life. And when I did that, I felt such perfect peace and perfect freedom."

A feeling of shame coursed through her at Logan's words. At one time, in spite of her antipathy to her father, she had a childlike faith in God. Had trusted Him to take care of her, much as she had trusted her parents to take care of her. She'd never had to worry about where her food or clothing was going to come from.

She thought of the decisions she had made in the past. She had made mistakes and had regretted some of them. She had spent so much time figuring out what she didn't want, she wasn't so sure anymore what she did want.

For the first time since she left the home she felt so stifled by, she yearned for the very things she had been spending all these years avoiding.

Security. Commitment. Love.

But she wasn't ready for them yet.

"But to go to church means to conform to what other people expect. To be exactly what they expect. Don't tell me that's freedom," she replied.

"My freedom in Christ has little to do with how other people see me," Logan said quietly, clasping his hands between his knees. "When I gave my life to Christ, I could stop trying to think I had to live for other people's expectations. I only had to please Him."

"And follow His commandments. Heavy responsibility."

"That's a response. A response of gratitude. Didn't

you ever do something just out of love? Just because you were so thankful for what you got?''

Guilt surged through her. She thought of the degree her father had paid for. The degree he had kept reminding her of. ''I've not always had the chance to be thankful. Usually I was told I had to be before I had a chance *to* be.''

Logan nodded. ''I'm starting to understand.''

''What? Me or my life?''

''Both, I think.'' He smiled at her, but then the sound of the girls finally returning caught their attention.

They had taken an inordinately long time to return, thought Sandra, wondering if this was part of the schemes Logan had alluded to.

''Hey, Uncle Logan, Sandra. We got your ice cream.''

Sandra welcomed the intrusion.

''Great, and you got just what I wanted,'' Logan said as they clomped up the stairs.

Brittany handed Logan his ice cream, her eyes flicking between them, a speculative gleam in her eye.

Sandra knew the truth of what happened between her and Logan would disappoint them mightily.

Yet as she took her ice cream from Bethany, she realized that while on the surface not much had happened, in reality much had.

Logan was getting closer to a part of her she'd not shown to too many people.

It made her vulnerable. It gave him power over her.

She wasn't sure what to think of it all.

Chapter Eleven

Sandra finished her cone and knew it was time for her to go home. So far the evening had been altogether too pleasant. Too much like a normal family, she thought, looking at the girls sitting at her feet.

She felt a wave of love and compassion for them as she thought of her mother. They had lost their mother at such a young age, they would only have a portion of the memories Sandra had.

Sandra wiped her fingers on the napkin Logan had provided as she glanced at him. She felt a flush warm her neck as she realized he had been watching her.

Again she couldn't look away. Again she wondered about this man. Wondered why he managed to make her talk about things she had never spoken about to anyone since she left home.

"I think the phone is ringing." Bethany cocked her head as if listening.

"I'll get it." Brittany surged to her feet and ran into the house, the door slapping on its frame behind her.

"It's for you, Uncle Logan." Her voice echoed from inside the house.

As Logan got up, Sandra couldn't help but wonder if maybe it was Karen.

None of your business, she chided herself. She glanced at her watch and knew it was time for her to go home. She had been here long enough.

She'd wait until Logan came back, then she'd leave, she decided. This whole scene was getting too domestic.

Logan came back, a frown creasing his forehead.

"What's the matter, Uncle Logan?" Bethany asked.

"That was Ian. My partner. There's been a problem with one of the projects we've been working on. I need to go back to Calgary. So that means you girls will have to come with me."

"No, Uncle Logan. Not yet," the girls cried.

Sandra felt her heart take a slow pitch downward.

She caught herself. Why should it matter to her? She couldn't look at him—wouldn't let him see that she felt anything at all.

But she could no more stop her eyes from darting to his than she could stop the spin of the earth on its axis.

Logan's gaze flicked from the twins to her, stopping, his lips pressed together as if displeased.

Did he want to stay?

Sandra pushed the thought aside. Of course he didn't. He had to get back to work. To making money.

"Can we please stay?" Brittany jumped to her feet.

Bethany was right behind. "We'll be good. We will. We'll listen to Sandra."

They clung to his hands, pleading.

"We can stay here. Sandra can stay with us." Brittany glanced at Sandra as if to confirm what she had said.

Sandra gave a noncommittal shrug, her eyes averted. She wasn't about to get caught up in this.

Logan sighed lightly, and in her peripheral vision she saw him plunge a hand through his thick hair, rearranging it. "I don't know, girls."

Sandra chanced a quick glance at him, and her eyes once again locked with his. She could see the question in them.

Don't do it, don't offer to stay. Keep your life separate.

But she was spending most of her day with these girls anyhow. What difference would a few evenings in the cabin make?

All the difference. You'll be giving them one more part of your life, the insidious voice in her head continued. *And then you'll be waiting for Logan to come back. Getting caught up with someone who's temporary in your life.*

"Sandra could stay with us, and take care of us," Bethany said quietly. She looked over her shoulder at Sandra. "Couldn't you?"

Sandra felt herself wavering as she met Bethany's soft blue eyes. "I don't know," she temporized, unwilling to say a flat-out no.

"Would you come back, Uncle Logan?" Brittany joined in the fray.

"I could." Logan spoke slowly, looking at Brittany. He took a slow breath, then looked at Sandra. "Would you be willing to stay?"

Sandra swallowed, glanced at the girls who were looking at her, their glances imploring her to consider it.

For their sake she should do it. If she didn't, Logan would have to take them to Calgary, and then he might decide to stay there. She wasn't quite ready to let the girls go yet.

That's not what it is, and you know it. It's him you don't want to let go of. Don't do it.

"Okay," she said quickly, as if taking her time answering might make her listen to the other voice in her mind. The reasonable one. "I'll stay with the girls."

They rushed to her side, throwing their arms around her. "Thank you, thank you. You're the best," they cried.

A peculiar warmth suffused her at the girls' enthusiastic thanks. At the feel of their arms holding her tight. Their hair was sun-warmed and smelled of shampoo. *Is this what it's like to have children?* she wondered. *Being held and thanked for doing so little. Giving part of myself away and getting all this back?*

"I think Sandra might like to breathe for a bit," Logan said dryly.

The girls pulled back, grins splitting their faces, and Sandra knew she had done the right thing. The easiest thing would have been to say no. To see them leave with Logan. And watch the three of them move out of her life.

She didn't want to think about that. Didn't have to. For the next few days, she was still a part of their lives. The reality of her situation was she had nowhere else to go. And until she paid for the shipment of glass, nothing else to do.

She wasn't ready to have Logan move out of her life so quickly. So unexpectedly. This way she could prepare to say goodbye.

"Well, I'd better get ready," Logan said, his thumbs slung in the belt loops of his pants. "Bethany, Brittany, I want you to get the guest bedroom ready for Sandra."

The girls grinned at each other and ran off, their excited giggles trailing in their wake.

"Well, you've just made two girls extremely happy," Logan said when the screen door had slapped shut behind them.

Sandra glanced at him and smiled. "It doesn't seem to take much," she said.

Logan's expression grew serious as he held her gaze. "I know how much it means to them to stay here," he said quietly. "It's been a crazy kind of holiday for them, what with catching up on schoolwork and all. But so far it's been working out okay. Thanks to you. I have to confess I had my reservations about you, but I want to thank you for making their schoolwork so interesting for them."

His words, his eyes holding hers, even his stance created an intimacy that felt so right, so real, Sandra had to catch herself from reaching out to him. From making a connection more tangible than the one they already shared.

Shocked and surprised at the feelings he elicited in her, Sandra looked down, fumbling for her crutches.

"I should go," she muttered, her heart pounding in her chest. "Tell the girls I'll see them in the morning."

In her awkwardness she dropped one of the crutches. Logan knelt beside her chair and picked it up.

"I'll walk you to your cabin," he said quietly as Sandra surged to her feet.

"That's fine. I'll be okay. It's not far. I'm used to the crutches." Her words tumbled out, mirroring her confusion. What was this man doing to her? Kissing her, complimenting her. Looking at her with those hazel eyes that made her forget all the differences between them.

Making her wonder if maybe, just maybe...

Sandra wrapped her hands around the crutches, squeezing them as if squeezing these ridiculous thoughts out of her mind.

"Thanks again for supper." She chanced a quick grin at him, wishing, praying for the composure she used to have around him.

"You're welcome, Sandra. I'm glad you could come." He slipped his hands in his pockets, as if he were waiting.

Then, with what she hoped was a nonchalant smile, Sandra started out, her crutches pounding a hollow beat on the deck.

Logan was right behind her as she navigated the stairs.

"I told you, I'll be okay." The words came out harsher than she had intended, but Logan didn't seem too perturbed.

"I'm sure you will, but I just like to make sure." And once again she was stumping along the street, Logan right beside her.

"I'll probably be gone tomorrow and part of the day

after. I'm sure I can get the business finished by then,'' he said quietly.

''And after that?'' Sandra couldn't stop the question. She needed to know.

''I had initially figured on staying here for two and a half weeks and then taking the tutor I had hired back to Calgary with me. But I'm going to have to make different plans.''

Sandra said nothing, knowing his plans didn't include her.

Spending time with Logan and the girls this evening had been more than pleasant. For the first time since her mother had died, Sandra had felt as if she was in a home, rather than a house.

For the first time in a long time she found herself attracted to a man who created a feeling of rightness in her.

She pushed the dangerous thought to the back of her mind. She had no right entertaining any kind of thoughts about Logan. They were too far apart in outlook, in attitude.

But should that matter?

They got to the door of Sandra's cabin. She thought he would leave then, but he opened the door for her and followed her inside.

The door closed behind him, and she turned to thank him again, disconcerted to see him standing directly in front of her. She had to tip her head back to look into his eyes. His deep, searching eyes.

''Thanks for bringing me home,'' she said, wishing she felt as nonchalant as she sounded.

"Just wanted to make sure you didn't hurt yourself," Logan said, smiling at her. "How's the knee?"

"It's fine."

"Really?"

"Well, there's no sense whining about it. The more you complain, the longer God lets you live."

Logan's smile widened at her flippant remark. "I guess you are feeling okay."

Sandra couldn't help but smile back. "Sorry. It's my defense mechanism," she admitted.

"I know." Logan's eyes held hers as the smile slowly faded from his mouth. He laid a warm hand on her shoulder, his fingers curling around it. "Are you sure you're going to be okay?"

Sandra wasn't sure at all. Not with the way he was looking at her right now. She couldn't stop her hand from reaching out to him. Resting on his chest.

Her heart climbed up her throat and then stopped when Logan lowered his mouth to hers.

Her crutches clattered to the ground as her arms slid around his neck. He was holding her, supporting her.

His hand tangled itself in her hair as he murmured her name against her mouth. Then a light sigh escaped his lips as he gently pulled away. He rested his forehead against hers. Sandra couldn't focus on his face. It was just a pale blur, his eyes two dark smudges.

"What's happening here, Sandra?" he murmured, his thumb stroking her neck.

Sandra didn't trust herself to respond. She didn't know herself. She had never felt this way with anyone. Ever. She had tried to tell herself again and again that Logan wasn't her type.

After this evening, however, standing within the safety of his arms, none of that mattered. Being with him felt good and true and right.

Logan dropped a light kiss on her forehead and drew back. Without a word he bent, picked up her crutches and handed them to her. "I better go," he said quietly, his forefinger tracing a light line down the side of her face.

Sandra was surprised at the feeling of deprivation that washed over her when he lowered his hand. Surprised at how incomplete she felt without him. It seemed an overreaction to such a simple thing. But she knew that between her and Logan, things weren't so simple anymore.

"Do you mind coming by at seven tomorrow morning? I want to get an early start" He slipped his hands into his pockets, still watching her.

She shook her head, hoping her voice sounded steadier than she felt. "I don't mind at all."

He smiled, and to Sandra it was like seeing the sun peeking through storm clouds. "I'll see you then."

And on that mundane comment, he walked out the door, leaving behind a distinctly bemused Sandra.

Sandra rolled over in her bed, glancing at the clock. Four o'clock. What had woken her? Her knee felt fine.

There it was again. A rustle, then the thunk of the kitchen door closing. Sandra sat up, her heart thudding in her chest, adrenaline coursing through her. Someone was trying to break in.

Then she heard a tuneless whistle, followed by a muttered question.

Cora was back.

Sandra eased herself out of bed and grabbed her crutches. She stumbled through the darkness toward the crack of light that appeared under her door.

Cora was standing in front of the fridge, one hand on the door, the other rooting through the precious few groceries Sandra had bought with the advance Logan had given her.

"Hey, Cora. What's up?" Sandra asked.

Cora whirled around, her hand pressed to her chest. "Sandra. You scared the living daylights out of me." Then she grinned at her friend. "What do you have to eat?"

Sandra helped Cora put a sandwich together. Cora made a pot of coffee, and they sat at the table.

Sandra found out that Cora hadn't found a job yet. "So I guess it's either head out east or maybe welfare," she said with a casual shrug.

"I thought we were going to try to make our own way in this world. Without help."

"My skills aren't appreciated," she mumbled around a mouthful of sandwich. "Hey, how's the stained glass business? You must have gotten some money."

Sandra explained what had happened as Cora finished the sandwich and made another. Sandra stifled a stab of annoyance at her friend's nonchalant attitude and how easily she helped herself to food that Sandra had paid for.

"I need some money for rent, Cora," Sandra said, crossing her arms on the table. This time she wasn't going to let Cora finesse her way out of paying her share.

"Well, if you're making money, then it's cool."

"No, it isn't cool, Cora. You owe me for gas on the way out here and rent for two months." Sandra frowned. "By the way, how did you get here?"

Cora held up her thumb with a grin. "Beats walking." She took another bite of her sandwich and jumped up. "Hey. Got some pictures."

And for the next half hour, the rent was conveniently forgotten. Sandra was regaled with stories of where Cora had been and some crazy notion of moving to the island where she could make a fortune growing ginseng. But as Sandra listened, she realized that where once she would have been entertained, she found that she grew annoyed with Cora's pipe dreams. Cora never managed to stay with anything longer than six weeks before she got impatient because the money didn't come in fast enough. Then she'd be off to the next thing.

"So, you gonna come?" Cora leaned forward, an expectant gleam in her eye. Sandra sat back, flipping through Cora's pictures, melancholy settling on her. At one time the idea of packing up and leaving might have created a sense of expectation and adventure, but now she knew different.

The excitement of the change would die down, and the new venture wouldn't live up to the high expectations, and Cora would start chafing. It took time to make money, and it never came easy.

"No. I'm not coming." Sandra handed the pictures back with a wry smile.

"Are you nuts?" Cora grabbed the pictures, shaking her head. "This is a great opportunity. The big chance."

"Yah. Just like selling my stained glass to Henri was a great opportunity. I'm still trying to get over that one."

"Okay. Tactical error. But at least you made some money. C'mon. It'll be fun. I mean, what's keeping you here?"

Sandra didn't want to tell her. Didn't want to share the fragile feelings that she knew had as much future as Cora's newest big chance did. "I've got this stained glass job to do," she said instead.

"And after that, why don't you come?"

Because you'll be somewhere else by then, Sandra thought. "I don't know what I'll do. Maybe get a job in Medicine Hat until I get other commissions."

"Don't be an idiot. You'll die of boredom. Like you always do." She looked at Sandra with a knowing smirk. "And I hate to burst your bubble, but you haven't really made as much money cutting glass as you thought you would."

Sandra shrugged Cora's comment away, knowing it for the truth. She swallowed a bubble of panic at the thought of trying, once again, to find out what she really wanted to do. Would she be able to work a steady job as she so casually mentioned to Cora?

But the other side of the coin was Cora and dreams and plans that never, ever came to fruition. Cora and scrimping and being forced to make bad decisions. All this for the sake of preserving a freedom that was illusionary.

And Sandra knew she didn't want to go back to that lifestyle. Not anymore.

"Anyhow, I'm going to bed," Sandra said, getting slowly to her feet. "I have to work tomorrow."

"I just got back," Cora grumbled. "Phone in sick. We need to catch up."

Sandra looked at her friend, remembering many times she had done just that. Sandra was the only one of the two who ever held down a traditional job, and Cora had always encouraged her to skip work. But this job was different. Brittany and Bethany were counting on her. She wasn't going to let them down.

"No. I'm going to work. I'll see you when I'm done."

Cora licked her fingers. "Maybe you will, maybe you won't."

Sandra held her friend's gaze, then shook her head. "If I don't, take care of yourself." Then she turned and hobbled to her bedroom. As she settled in the bed, she realized that not once had Cora asked her what happened to her knee.

"Here's where I'll be staying." Logan handed Sandra a piece of paper. "This is the number of the condo, this one is the office's."

He looked at her bent head as she glanced at the paper. She wore a long skirt today. The same one she had worn the first time she had come here, he realized.

"Thanks. I'm hoping I won't need this," Sandra said, glancing at him. She gave a little hop and pinned the paper to the bulletin board that served as a message board beside the fridge. Logan had to catch himself from reaching out to make sure she didn't fall.

He'd had to stop himself a number of times this morning from supporting her, helping her up the stairs. It was as if he was looking for an excuse to touch her, to make sure she was real. To show himself what happened last night and the night before that wasn't just loneliness, but emotions that might, just might, have a future.

He glanced at the clock. He had to get going, but he was loath to leave. Ian's timing really stunk, yet at the same time being away from Sandra might be just what Logan needed to put her into perspective.

"Will you be back for supper tomorrow night?" she asked, tossing her hair from her face as she turned to him, resting on her crutches.

Logan shook his head, a wistful tenderness engulfing him. He couldn't stop himself this time and reached out to gently stroke a strand of hair from her face. He didn't want to go, he thought with a sudden yearning as his fingers drifted down her cheek.

He drew in a deep breath, as if to dispel the notion, then dropped his hand and took a step back.

He really needed some time out, he thought, shaken by his reaction to her.

"I'm not sure when I'll be back tomorrow, but it will be later on in the evening."

Sandra nodded, looking down. He waited a moment, as if willing her to look at him, but she kept her eyes resolutely on a point beyond him, just below his shoulders.

He turned and caught a glimpse of two heads quickly

withdrawing from the doorway and knew the girls had been spying on them. The thought disconcerted him. If they had seen that slight interaction between him and Sandra, no telling how far their imaginations would run with it.

But there was nothing he could do about that now.

He affected a casual air and sauntered into the main living area. "You girls listen to Sandra, now," he said, holding their gaze. "I don't want to hear about any funny business while I'm gone."

They shook their heads, watching him with shrewd eyes. "We'll be good," Bethany said, giving him a quick hug.

Logan returned the hug, rubbed Brittany's hair and with a quick wave he left.

But as he drove away, he wondered how he would feel about Sandra on his return.

Chapter Twelve

"Why can't we go to the beach now?" Brittany looked up at Sandra, her tone wheedling, her eyes wide with innocence.

"Because we're not finished yet. That's why." Sandra pushed the textbook toward Brittany and opened it again.

"But we can work on this tonight. Uncle Logan isn't here," Bethany added.

"That's no excuse." Sandra frowned at the more docile of the twins, surprised at the disgruntled attitude that had come over her since Logan had left. "You still have to get the day's work done."

Brittany let out a sigh like a gust of wind. "We've been working all year already. Now we have to work all summer. It's just not fair."

Sandra could sympathize. And a few weeks ago, she might have sided with the girls. However, after spending two weeks with them she noticed they both had a tendency to put off what they could.

Logan had been correct. They needed to learn a measure of self-discipline.

The thought of him made her heart wobble. In every quiet moment the memory of his kiss, of his light touch this morning came back with a rush of wonderment and concern. Why was he doing this? And why was she letting it happen? They were worlds apart, yet something drew them together. Something as elemental as loneliness and as basic as a few kisses.

But Sandra knew it was more.

"We could work really hard tomorrow and get it done then," Brittany continued, taking Sandra's momentary lapse in concentration as assent.

Sandra pulled herself back with a jerk, castigating herself for woolgathering. She was acting as silly and as abstracted as a young woman in love. As if she hadn't learned a few hard lessons in that department.

"No, Brittany," she said, hoping she sounded firm. "Once a person starts procrastinating, you're never done."

"But this stuff is boring, and I thought you told us that life should never be boring."

Sandra felt an unwelcome jolt as her words came back to her. "Well, guess what?" Sandra said with a wide grin. "Sometimes I'm wrong. And you are going to find that finishing something boring can make you feel good about yourself. Now let's get back to work."

Both girls let out sighs, and Sandra had to stifle hers. It was a struggle each day to make their lessons not only relevant but interesting. As a result the girls seemed to think that Sandra was there more to entertain than to teach them.

What had made her change her view?

Logan had, Sandra thought. Logan as well as Cora. After spending time with Logan and the girls, Cora was such a contrast. It was as if she saw her friend clearly for the first time. And by doing so, got a look at herself and where she might be headed.

Brittany shut the book Sandra had pushed her way. ''I thought that when Uncle Logan left you would be easier on us,'' she said with a pout.

''Well, you were wrong,'' she said with a quick grin. ''Now back to work.''

The rest of the day didn't go much better. By the time supper was over and the dishes were finally done, Sandra had gained a new appreciation and respect for Logan.

She also realized that the girls were far better behaved around him than around her.

She went through another struggle to get the girls to bed at a decent time. But finally they were cleaned up and tucked into their beds.

''Are you going to do our devotions with us?'' Bethany asked, her hands folded demurely across her chest.

Sandra glanced at the book that lay on the bedside table between the two girls. ''Sure,'' she said with a nonchalance she didn't feel.

Today had been enough of an epiphany, she thought as she picked up the book. She wasn't sure she needed any further reminders of how wrong her life had been.

But she settled on Bethany's bed, paging through the book until she found the bookmark. At the top of the page was the Bible verse. She read it out loud, a slow ache building at the words from Psalm 90.

May the favor of the Lord our God rest upon us; establish the work of our hands for us—yes, establish the work of our hands.

And what had her hands done that God could establish? she wondered as she paused to swallow past the thickness in her throat. At one time it wouldn't have mattered as much to her, but a different reality had permeated her life.

Logan and his solid trust in God.

Logan and his penetrating questions that had worn down her defenses against people just like him. Logan and the easy way he spoke to God.

"Aren't you going to read?" Bethany asked, sitting up.

Sandra took a deep breath to still her fluctuating emotions and nodded. But the devotional piece hit her even harder than the verses did. It spoke of God-given talents and responsibilities to use those talents. A year ago she might have scoffed at what she read. But the past year had been difficult. Her pride had struggled with her conscience and her knowledge of God.

She finished the piece then listened to the girls' prayers. They prayed for their grandmother, for their uncle Logan and thanked the Lord for the day. Listening to their confidently spoken requests, she harkened back to the time in her life when she would list her own requests with a simple faith that God would take care of her.

And He had.

She just hadn't done much with what He had given her, she realized as she got to her feet.

"Can you kiss us good-night?" Brittany asked as

Sandra turned off the bedroom light. "Uncle Logan always does."

With a forced smile Sandra hobbled to the bed, bent and gave Brittany a gentle kiss on her forehead. As she looked at the young girl, her heart warmed. She did the same for Bethany.

"Sleep tight, girls," she whispered, a feeling of completeness surging through her.

Sandra paused in the doorway, looking at the girls, but in her mind she saw Logan's tall form bent over the beds. Her heart flipped, and a curious ache squeezed her heart. Did these girls know how fortunate they were? Logan, who took such good care of them, could just as easily have handed the responsibility to their grandmother.

And then where would they be?

Traipsing around Alaska waiting for inspiration, that's where. Falling even further behind in their schoolwork. She had always maintained that formal education was overrated, but thanks to her education, she had a paying job.

Something she'd not had in a while.

The next day the girls weren't quite as rambunctious, but they still tested her. Sandra had her hands full, keeping them focused and under control.

Lunchtime drifted by, and for the rest of the afternoon, Sandra found herself tensing each time she heard a vehicle. She was waiting for Logan, she realized, catching herself glancing out the window for what must have been the fifth time in an hour.

The afternoon dragged on leaden feet. When they

were done they went for a quick swim. Supper was simple. Leftovers from the night before.

They were just finishing the dishes when Sandra heard the faint purr of a vehicle pull up to the front door, then stop.

"Uncle Logan is home," the girls called. They ran out of the kitchen, their dish towels fluttering to the floor in their wake.

Sandra's heart gave a curious lurch, her hands felt suddenly cold, and she had trouble swallowing.

Logan was home.

She bit her lip and pressed her eyelids shut, squeezing away the errant emotions. Logan was her boss. The uncle of her students. Straitlaced and narrow-minded.

Then why had she missed him? Missed his slightly hovering presence, the way he could dominate a room just by standing in the doorway. Missed the way his hazel eyes could hold hers, draw her in.

Pulling herself together, she carefully bent to pick up the towels the girls dropped, making sure she didn't bend her knee. Fitting the crutches under her arms, she followed the girls to the doorway.

"Hey, Uncle Logan," they called waving at him.

"Hey, yourselves," he returned.

Through the open door, over the shoulders of the twins, she watched as he got out of the van and tossed his sunglasses onto his seat. He was wearing a suit, which sat easily on his shoulders. A dark tie cinched the collar of his white shirt, giving him an austere air.

Sandra felt a heaviness in her chest where her heart was. Unreachable, that's what he was. In another world and another place that she had been running away from. A place she couldn't go back to. Not without getting pulled into the vortex of past expectations.

Logan reached into the back, pulled out his suitcase and strode up the walk toward them.

"So how have you been doing?"

Bethany was the first to reach his side, slipping her arm easily through his. "We did all our work."

Brittany was on the other side, relieving him of his suitcase. "And we finished supper. Did you have some?"

"I ate already." He tousled their hair and pulled them close to him, dropping a kiss first on Bethany then Brittany's head.

And Sandra felt a sharp stab of jealousy at their easy rapport. At how nonchalant the girls were about the affection Logan so quickly bestowed on them.

They walked up the stairs and came to a stop in front of Sandra.

She got a smile that did nothing for her composure and a faint wink that made her cling to her crutches in surprise.

"Hi there, Sandra. How are you?"

Simple words. Words she had heard so many times, but hearing Logan speak them gave her a peculiar thrill.

"I'm okay."

"And your knee?" He glanced at her crutches, then at her face, his eyes holding hers just as she remembered.

"It's okay, too."

This was scintillating conversation, she thought wryly, but somehow she couldn't conjure up a humorous comment, a snappy quip. She felt as tongue-tied as any teenage girl in the presence of her crush.

"I'll just go change," he said with another grin. He gave the girls a quick hug and left.

Sandra and the girls settled into the main room, leaving the recliner for Logan.

He was back in record time, his suit replaced with faded blue jeans and a T-shirt.

The heaviness in Sandra's chest drifted away at the sight of his casual clothes. This was a more approachable Logan.

He dropped into the recliner and let out a gusty sigh as he raised the footrest. "Oh, it's good to be off the road," he said, closing his eyes.

The girls sat perched on the edge of the couch, their eyes darting warily from Sandra to Logan, as if looking for any sign that their work had not been in vain.

It hadn't, thought Sandra, with a peculiar hitch in her chest. Being away from Logan and then seeing him again had created a shift in her perception of him, in her feelings toward him.

And don't forget the kisses.

Sandra felt her cheeks flush. She didn't want to feel this way, knew it shouldn't happen. Her and Logan. They were just too different.

And yet...

She glanced at him and caught his steadfast gaze. It was as if his eyes could see what she didn't want to acknowledge.

Her attraction to him.

"Did you finish what you needed to?" she asked,

aware that the twins weren't going to contribute to this conversation at all.

Knowing them, they were probably planning their escape so Logan and Sandra could be conveniently alone.

"It went okay." Logan's deep voice, now familiar, seemed to surround her.

Sandra didn't know how to respond to that. She glanced at the twins again, but they were determinedly quiet.

"Girls, maybe your uncle would like something to drink?"

Brittany jumped up and grabbed her sister by the arm, "Some soda or orange juice?" she asked as she pulled Bethany toward the kitchen,

"Orange juice," Logan said with a wry grin.

The girls left, and Logan and Sandra were alone.

They glanced at each other and then away. Sandra scrabbled through her mind, trying to come up with something, anything.

Logan sat up and lowered the footrest.

Sandra swallowed as he got to his feet. What was he going to do?

"Here's your orange juice, Uncle Logan." Bethany came into the room, concentrating on the glass of juice in her hands. She looked up, her steps faltered and she almost dropped the glass. She set it carefully on the end table beside Logan's recliner and darted a quick look over her shoulder. "I think I'm tired," she announced.

Brittany came up behind her with a plate of cookies and frowned at her sister. Then her glance ticked over

Logan and Sandra, and she nodded. "Me, too. I think we should go to bed."

"I just got home," Logan said, biting one corner of his lip.

The barely subdued sparkle in his eye showed Sandra he knew the girls were up to their usual tricks. And the grin that slowly spread across his face showed her he didn't seem to mind one bit.

"You and Sandra can come and tuck us in, if you want."

Sandra caught Logan's helpless look. "I guess, if Sandra wants."

But Sandra remembered last night too clearly. And because of her changing feelings toward Logan, she wasn't too sure she was ready for another reminder from the Lord in the form of the twins' evening devotions.

"I'll just stay here," she said. "I should leave pretty soon, anyhow."

Logan held her eyes, his expression softening. Her heart gave a funny little quiver, and she looked away. This was getting ridiculous, she thought, pleating the material of her loose skirt as he went upstairs.

She should leave right now. Things had already gone further than she could deal with.

She heard water running and the faint rumble of Logan's voice, the excited voices of the girls. Then a cry of dismay, and Logan was speaking again.

She wondered what he had to tell them. Wondered what they might find to complain about this time. She really had to go, she thought. Whatever was building between her and Logan, if indeed anything was, it was a waste of time. He was leaving next week and she at the end of the month. Her rent was paid up until then, and after that she had to come up with a new plan. But what?

She didn't know what was supposed to come next.

"Well, I think the girls are settled for the night," Logan said, coming down the stairs. "They said they were very tired." He stopped in front of Sandra, his thumbs slung in the front belt loops of his pants. "What do you think?"

Sandra looked at him, the banked gleam in his eye quickening her pulse. "I think that they are very choosy about which reality they are going to select."

"I just hope they don't select sneaking out again."

"Well, I'm here. And I was the one they were sneaking out to see." Sandra forced a smile to her face as the memory of that night came crashing back.

"That night seems like a long time ago instead of just a couple of weeks," he said softly.

Sandra felt a fragment of fear shiver through her.

He was right. In the past few days much had changed, and yet nothing had. She was still a temporary fixture in his life, and he in hers.

The atmosphere was beginning to feel charged, and Sandra was eager to dispel it, yet not so eager to go home just yet.

"The girls were telling me about your project—that you were having some difficulty with it. Did you get it done?"

Logan shook his head, dropping to the couch beside her. He lay his head back and laced his fingers over his stomach, his mouth pursed in a wry grin. "Nope.

Just can't seem to get it.'' He rolled his head to face her. ''But I've decided I'm not going to obsess over it. If I get it I get it, if I don't…'' He lifted his hands off his stomach in a gesture of resignation. ''God has never failed to take care of me yet.''

Sandra reached for sarcasm, her best defense against the rash of feelings this man brought out in her. ''My goodness. Full speed ahead to prosperity, and Logan Napier is going to let a chance for fame and fortune slip through his fingers.''

Logan shook his head lightly, laughing. ''You know me better than that.''

His voice was low, almost caressing, and Sandra felt all the unraveling ends of her life slowly become whole in his presence.

''Yes,'' she agreed. ''I do.'' She looked away. ''But I'd still like to see the drawings you've been working on.''

Logan sighed. ''Okay. You asked for it.'' He pushed himself from the couch and left. He soon came back holding a sheaf of papers. ''I've been fooling with a number of ideas, but l can't say I'm really thrilled with any of them.'' He shuffled through the papers and gave Sandra a quizzical glance over the top of them. ''You realize I'm making myself totally vulnerable to that sharp tongue of yours by doing this.''

Sandra held his gaze and gave him a careful smile. ''I'll be gentle,'' she said.

Then he gave her the papers, and she felt as if something fine and delicate had shifted between them.

He sat beside her as she went through the sheaf of papers. Sandra was impressed with his expertise.

Somehow the drawings she saw didn't mesh with the straightforward image Logan presented.

"So, what's wrong with them?" she asked, turning back to the first page.

Logan took the pages from her and studied them, his elbows resting on his knees.

"They look like every single house in Calgary, that's what."

Sandra angled her head as if to get a better look. This brought her closer to Logan. Fine shivers danced up her arm at his proximity.

"Not really." She temporized and cleared her throat. "What do these people want?" *Keep the topic safe,* she reminded herself.

"They want it built into the hill so that you can only see part of it when you come onto the yard." Logan showed her another view, and Sandra had to keep herself from catching her breath. Even though it was just lines on paper, she could see that this was going to be an impressive home.

"I'm going with flying buttresses between these pillars to hold back the lateral load. There's going to be a lot of concrete because the soil is quite sandy."

Sandra nodded, trying to look knowledgeable, but when Logan glanced sidelong at her, his smile told her she wasn't succeeding.

"Anyhow, it looks cold and austere and I don't know how to soften it." Logan shuffled through the papers once more, slowly shaking his head. "If the Jonserads had a clear idea of what they wanted, it would be easier. Mrs. Jonserad kept talking about light and air and space, and all Mr. Jonserad wanted was a room he could smoke cigars in."

Sandra's laugh bubbled up. "So she needs the space to get rid of the cigar smoke."

"I guess." He scratched his head.

Sandra gently tugged on the top piece of paper. "Do you mind?" she asked, holding out her other hand for the pencil she knew Logan always carried in his pocket.

He gave it to her, and with another quick glance to him for permission, she took his initial rendering and squinted at it. Then she turned it sideways and held it up. She looked at it from all possible angles.

"What about if you soften this part of the house?" she asked, pointing with the pencil at the front entrance. "Put in a curved window."

"It wouldn't work with the other lines," Logan said, leaning closer. "I've done the math."

"Oh, you and your math," she chided with a light smile. "You have to learn to let go and let your creativity flow."

"You sound like my mother."

"That's good. She's a very creative person."

"A lackadaisical person." Logan huffed.

"She wasn't always wrong, you know. As I said before, she raised you, and you turned out just fine."

Logan grinned. "You think?" He turned serious. "You may be right. But I know I am, too. Your father wasn't all wrong, either."

Sandra held his gaze, sensing the seriousness of the moment. But she couldn't hold his eyes. She looked at the drawing. "It would work if you repeated the idea here." She drew a few quick strokes on each end of the house.

"That looks good. But from a construction viewpoint, it would be a nightmare to work in. Raises the costs substantially without enough aesthetic gain." He held out his hand, and without a word, she handed him the pencil. He made a few corrections.

"How about this?" She took the pencil, but as she drew, she poked a hole in the paper. "Oh, no. I'm sorry."

"No, no. Don't worry," Logan reassured her. "Let's go sit at the table. It'll be easier."

They moved and continued working, bouncing ideas off each other. Sandra didn't have the first clue about architecture or construction. When Logan started talking about sheet pilings, rebar and angle of repose she was lost.

What she did recognize was the energy flowing between the two of them as slowly the rendering began to change.

Logan grew excited, nodding as she made suggestions.

He got a fresh pad of sketch paper and started over again.

"I wonder if a stained glass window would work in here," Sandra suggested. "Mrs. Jonserad did mention that she wanted to work with light."

Logan angled her a sly, sidewise look. "A little plug for your own business?" he teased.

Sandra shrugged, feeling her face warm. "Maybe. But I like the idea."

"I do, too." Logan pursed his lips as he considered

it. "That could work. If we go with a modern concept to echo the basic design of the house."

Logan made a few quick lines, grinning as he did so. "This is great," he enthused, the front view of the home taking shape as he sketched. "Look, I think this would work." He finished and laid the paper down, as if to have a better look at it. Then he slung an arm over Sandra's shoulders. "Wow. I'm really impressed."

Sandra let him pull her against him, allowing them this moment of closeness. Just a few moments, she promised herself, letting his warmth and strength fill the empty spots of her life. She closed her eyes as if to concentrate on the moment, to store it in a place where she might take it out later on. When Logan was out of her life.

Then, just as she was about to pull away, Logan shifted his weight and with his free hand cupped her chin.

Her eyes flew open in time to see him lower his head. Then his face became a blur as his lips touched hers, warm and inviting. Sandra couldn't stop her hands from slipping around his neck, her fingers from tangling themselves in his thick hair. She knew she should pull away, stop this, but her lonely heart, her empty soul hungered for all she knew Logan was and all she knew he could give her.

Logan touched his lips to her forehead, her hair.

She bent her head and slowly lowered her hands. A careful withdrawal.

Logan sat back, his hands toying with her fingers.

"Now what, Sandra?" he asked, his voice husky. "Where do we go from here?"

She couldn't answer his question because she didn't know. She had only known him a few weeks, but tonight she had felt a connection with him that was as old as the earth.

"I thought being away from you for a few days would help put things into perspective," Logan said, his thumb tracing a path across the back of her hand. He looked at her then, his gaze direct, unyielding. "I didn't expect that I would miss you."

Once again Sandra couldn't look away, and once again she didn't want to.

He had missed her.

Why did those simple words from this particular man make her heart sing? They shouldn't, she reminded herself. She shouldn't be letting herself get caught up in this man and his life. They were too different. She didn't know what she wanted, whereas he knew exactly where he was headed.

It would never work.

Chapter Thirteen

Logan stared at Sandra's bent head and wondered what was happening to him.

He slipped his thumbs over Sandra's hands again, his mind arguing with his heart. Nothing had changed in their lives. They had merely gotten to know each other better.

Yet he knew—sensed that Sandra felt a dissatisfaction with her life. He remembered something she had said just before he left—"I lost my way."

He thought of what he had found out this afternoon. He knew he had to tell Sandra.

"I, uh, got a message from my secretary." Logan kept his hold on her hands, unsure what to hope for. What to pray for. "She found a tutor for me who's willing to start Monday and work for the rest of the summer."

He felt Sandra's slight withdrawal, the gentle tug of her hands. But he didn't let go. He had more to say.

He looked at her, wishing she would do the same.

"But I was going to ask you if you could come with us to Calgary. If you'd be willing to work for me there."

It was a long shot. Maybe even a dumb suggestion.

All he knew was that it took only a few hours away from her to make him realize how much she had come to mean to him. He wasn't sure where this would go, he only knew that somehow he wasn't ready to let her leave.

"I don't know," Sandra replied, her voice unsteady.

It wasn't what he hoped to hear, but he knew Sandra well enough to know she wasn't going to commit to something like this immediately.

"I have a friend who's away for the month of August on a project. He always told me that if I could find someone to live in his condo, that would be great. You'd have a place to stay and a place to finish your lamps. Maybe even find another job."

He realized he was pressuring her, pushing her into a corner. But he wanted to make sure that all the options and possibilities were laid out before she made a decision.

Sandra looked at him, her eyes holding his in a long look that cut directly to his heart. "I'd like to think about this."

Logan nodded. Of course she couldn't make a decision right away. They both realized the portent of what he was suggesting. "I understand. But I need to tell you that no matter what you decide, the girls and I are leaving tomorrow night."

Another absent nod from Sandra. Then she finally

succeeded in pulling her hands out of his. "I should go," she whispered, looking around for her crutches.

Logan picked them up and handed them to her as she rose. She wouldn't look at him. Wouldn't make eye contact.

He wished there was some way he could understand what was going through her mind.

"You don't have to walk me home," she said, moving toward the door.

Logan ignored that remark as he held the door open for her and followed her into the cool of the evening.

As they made their way to her house, Logan felt as if he'd made himself vulnerable to her by offering her the job. It was like an echo of the approval he kept hoping he would get from his parents for what he was doing.

But what else could he have done? he wondered. He couldn't just leave her. Not after discovering how much he missed her. He gave Sandra a quick sidewise glance, surprised to see her looking directly at him.

"What are you thinking about?" He couldn't help asking.

Sandra smiled lightly, then looked ahead. "I'm thinking that those two girls may not have parents, but they are the luckiest girls I've met."

"Why do you say that?"

"Because they have an uncle who looks out for them. Who takes good care of all aspects of their lives. I know that's not how I talked a few weeks ago," Sandra continued, stopping at the end of her walk. She shook her thick hair, glancing at him. "You're a good man, Logan Napier. And you've done a good job with Brittany and Bethany."

Even as her compliment warmed his heart, her words sounded suspiciously like words of farewell. A tying off of loose ends.

In the diffused light of evening, her eyes were like dark smudges in her face. Unreadable and mysterious.

Logan wanted to touch her, to establish some kind of connection, but sensed that this was not the time or place. He would see her tomorrow, he reasoned. She hadn't given him a definite answer one way or the other. He had to bide his time.

And trust.

"Thanks for that, Sandra," he said quietly, rocking on his heels. "And I'll see you tomorrow." He couldn't stop himself from reaching out, brushing his knuckle over her cheek. Then he left.

Sandra watched him go, wavering between calling him back and keeping her mouth shut. His offer of a job was a turning point in their relationship. A change that would take her irrevocably in another direction. Could she go?

Could she stay here when the thought of him and the girls leaving created a dull ache in her chest, a sense of losing something pure and real?

Yet to go with them would mean going back to Calgary, the place her father lived. She wasn't ready for him and wanted to see him on her own terms. She had dreamed so many times of being able to show him that she could make it on her own. That she didn't need the degree he had forced her to get.

She wanted to prove that her choices were valid. That she could finish what she started and make money doing it.

Going to Calgary as the girls' tutor was not what she had planned. But she knew it could lead to more than she was able and maybe even willing to give Logan and his nieces.

Sandra pushed open the door of her cabin. Cora was draped all over their couch, papers scattered around her. She looked up and grinned as Sandra entered.

"I decided to stay for a couple of days. I need a base of operations for now."

Sandra nodded. *And you needed something to eat,* she thought.

"And how was your day of coaxing young girls into streamlined learning processes?" Cora asked.

"It went well." Sandra sat down in the lumpy chair across from the sofa.

"And I noticed that a very good-looking man escorted you to the door." Cora grinned at Sandra and tucked a pencil behind her ear.

"The girls' uncle. My boss." Sandra said the words as much for herself as for Cora.

Does a boss stroke your cheek when he says goodnight? Does he kiss you like Logan did?

Sandra could feel the heat rising up her neck and warming her cheeks at the very thought of Logan. But fortunately Cora was too busy making some notations on one of the papers scattered in front of her to notice.

"So how long are you going to work for him?"

"He and the girls are going to Calgary tomorrow night."

"Hey, did you know that Jane is in Calgary now? I saw her. She said hey and gave me her number." Cora fished in the pocket of her pants and pulled out a card. "If you're going there you can look her up. I think she's looking for a roommate."

Sandra took the card. "I don't think I'm going to Calgary," she said. "He found a tutor there."

Cora pulled a face. "Lousy luck for you, girl. Two jobs lost in one evening."

Sandra frowned. "What do you mean, two jobs?"

Cora got up and handed Sandra a piece of paper with a scribbled message on it. "I took this phone call earlier today."

Sandra read it. Quickly at first. Then once again as the words slowly sank in, heavy and hard.

The restaurant that had requested her lamps had changed ownership. The new owner didn't feel obligated to keep the contract. So he was canceling the order.

Sandra thought of all the materials she had sitting in the little room that served as her workshop. All the money they represented.

The failure this represented. Another job she wouldn't be able to finish.

She carefully folded the paper, futility washing over her like a wave.

You're a failure. Nothing but a failure.

The harsh and painful words her father threw at her as she left home echoed through her mind.

He was right.

"So, what are you going to do?" Cora asked.

Sandra ran her finger along the sharp edge of the paper, wishing Cora was gone. Wishing she was alone.

"I don't know."

"You thought any more about coming with me?"

Sandra looked across the table at Cora, glanced at the papers she had scattered around her. How many times since she met Cora had she seen the same scenario? Cora full of plans and schemes. None of them successful.

And she was no better, she realized.

You started with a no to your family. That doesn't take you anywhere, if you don't know what you are going to say yes to.

Logan's words sifted through her mind. He was so right. Her decisions had been made as responses, rather than as beginnings.

Please, Lord. Show me what I should do.

The prayer was involuntary, but even as she formulated the words, she knew the answer.

"I'm not going," she said firmly.

"What?" Cora stood up, shaking her head. "What else are you going to do?"

"I don't know, but I'm going to figure out my own life." She wasn't quite sure how, she just had a feeling that she had to start making normal plans.

With what? Guidance from God?

Maybe.

Sandra endured an instant of pain at the thought of Logan. At the thought of the girls he was trying to raise to be responsible citizens.

Unlike her.

"I'm going to bed," she told Cora. "I'll see you in the morning."

Cora held her gaze, as if testing her, then with a casual shrug looked away. "Sure thing."

It took Sandra no time to wash up, but as she lay in bed alone, sorrow engulfed her. Sorrow and the haunting reality that once again she had to start over.

Sandra slowed as she came closer to Logan's cabin. This morning she had almost chickened out and written a note.

But last night she had made a decision to make changes in her life. And one of the changes was to face things head-on instead of running away.

Talking to Logan face to face was part of the deal, she figured.

She had gone over every possibility in her mind. Had tried to reason everything out. But it all came back to the fact that the independent life she thought she had carved out for herself was a sham. The news Cora had given her yesterday only underlined the total failure of her plans.

Of her life. And she knew it wasn't fair to Logan to pretend that she had anything to offer him.

Sandra took a slow breath, sent up a quick prayer for strength and worked her way up the stairs. She didn't need the crutches anymore and had decided to bring them to Logan. He knew where they had come from and would probably return them for her.

She raised her hand to knock on the door.

Don't do it, just leave. He doesn't have to know.
You'll never see them again.

But she had done enough of that. She knew that she cared too much for him to just walk away. Sandra swallowed a knot of pain that formed in her chest.

Please, Lord, help me get through this.

She knocked on the door, hard. From inside the cabin she heard a flurry of steps and then the twins were at the door, grinning at her with expectation.

"So, you gonna come with us?" Bethany asked.

Sandra smiled at the girls, the knot getting larger. She had truly come to care for these two. Had enjoyed, more than she thought she would, the challenge of teaching them.

"Is your uncle Logan up yet?" she managed to ask, pleased that her voice sounded so normal as she avoided answering Bethany.

"Of course he is." Brittany's voice held a note of surprise that Sandra had to ask.

"I thought he might be sleeping in, that's all."

Brittany rolled her eyes. "As if. I don't think he went to bed at all last night." Then she grinned at Sandra. "But he's not grumpy. Come in."

Sandra limped through the door. *Now what?* she thought. *Sit? Stand? How long is it going to take to tell Logan what I've decided?*

"Hi there." Logan entered the room, a pencil stuck behind his ear, a smile creasing his unshaven face. His rumpled shirt was tucked into faded blue jeans. His feet were bare. The overall effect was a complete contradiction to the very put-together Logan she knew.

His hazel eyes lit briefly as they held hers, then he glanced at his clothes. "Sorry about this. I was busy

most of the night.'' He gestured to her. ''Come. I want
to show you something.''

Against her will, Sandra walked slowly to the room
where he worked, the girls trailing behind her.

''Look, I think I got it.'' Logan was bent over his
drafting table, sorting through the papers there. He
pulled one out, turned and handed it to her.

Sandra didn't look at him, but concentrated fiercely
on the heavy paper she held. The house she saw there
took her breath away. Elegant yet welcoming. A har-
mony of windows and angles softened by a large, half-
round stained glass window echoed by two smaller
ones flanking it. It was a home as well as a statement.

''It's beautiful,'' she whispered.

Logan was beside her. Sandra could feel the warmth
of his arm as it brushed hers. She felt her eyes begin
a dangerous prickling and knew that if she didn't pull
herself together she was going to cry.

''I didn't get it right until you helped me,'' he said
quietly, his deep voice beside her creating a circle of
intimacy that excluded the girls, who were avidly ignoring the two of them. ''I wish I could tell you how
much I appreciate it.''

Sandra bit her lip, handing him the paper. ''I didn't
do anything, Logan.'' She blinked carefully, thankful
that no tears escaped. ''I just doodled. You're the one
with the talent and the ideas.'' She gave him a weak
smile, wishing she could tell him and go. Wishing he
wouldn't look at her with those warm hazel eyes that
promised so much.

Promised her what she didn't deserve. She was exactly what he had initially said she was, she thought,

looking away. Irresponsible and selfish. She had taken an education from her father, and even though she had tried to send him what money she could spare, it would have barely paid the interest on any loan she would have had to take out. She had this job with Brittany and Bethany thanks to that education.

"Look, I've thought about your offer," she said quickly before she changed her mind. "It's great, and I'd love to continue working with the girls...." Her voice faltered, and she took a slow breath, wondering how she was going to tell him. "But I've got other plans and—" she lifted her shoulder in a faint shrug, chancing a quick look at him "—I don't think it would work."

Surprising how thoroughly a face could change expression without moving many muscles, she thought, watching Logan's features alter from open friendliness to reserved animosity.

The girls cried out, but a quick glance from Logan silenced them. He could do that so easily, Sandra thought. He had much better control over the girls than she ever could hope to. He, who claimed to have no stability in his life, had more than she did. And she, who had been raised by dependable parents and put through school, was rootless and drifting. Each thought dismantled the life she thought she had built for herself.

A life with no foundation, she thought with a throb of sorrow. A selfish life built on sand.

What could she possibly give this man?

"What do you mean, you don't think it would work?" Logan asked.

This was harder than she had anticipated. Sandra held his angry gaze, and as usual took refuge in humor.

"You know me," she said lightly. "I'm just here until I can find a really good fast-food job."

"And that's your ambition?" Logan shook his head. "I think I know you better than that."

His unexpected defense almost wore her down. But she knew she had to stay firm. She didn't deserve Logan. Didn't deserve the steady, caring person he was.

"Well, you know what they say about ambition. It's just a poor excuse for not having enough sense to be lazy." She forced another smile, then began walking out the door. She had to go. The longer she stayed, the weaker her resolve.

She knew that something was happening between her and Logan. Intrinsically she knew he wasn't the flirting type. He had kissed her, had held her, and she had responded to him. He was growing more and more important to her.

And so were those dear, exasperating, sweet girls.

But they all deserved better than what she had to offer.

Brittany and Bethany were beside her, hanging on to her, pleading with her. She stopped, wishing they would leave.

"Sandra." Logan said her name. Against her better judgment, she turned to him.

He stood facing her, his hands on his hips, chewing on one corner of his mouth. He laughed, a short, bitter sound. "So this is it? You're just going to walk away? No explanations, no solid reason."

How much had changed, she thought, unable to hold

his angry gaze. "When I took this job on I knew it was only going to be temporary." She chanced a quick look at him. "And so did you."

"Yeah. I guess that's true." He shook his head, then laughed again. "I owe you for this week yet," he said. "Let me write you out a check."

Sandra wanted this to be done but also knew that she would need the money he was going to give her, so she waited.

He yanked open a drawer and pulled out a checkbook. He filled the check in and ripped it out of the book, handing it to her without looking up.

Sandra took it, then Logan held out his hands to the girls. "C'mon, Bethy. Brit. Let Sandra go."

Sandra watched them walk to Logan's side. Where they belonged.

Without a look behind her she walked slowly out of the cabin, down the steps and to her home.

She didn't want to think about him. Didn't want to wonder what his opinion of her was. He was out of her life, she out of his.

But as she paused by the door of her cabin, her heart a heavy stone in her chest, she knew she would never forget him.

Chapter Fourteen

"Come on down, girls." Logan called up the stairs. "We're ready to leave."

He and the girls had spent most of the morning packing their clothes, personal items and any groceries they had into the van. He had originally planned to stay another day. To go to church. In some optimistic part of his mind he had hoped he might talk Sandra into coming with them.

He leaned against the stairs' handrail a moment, surprised at the dull ache created by the thought of her. Sandra, as she had told him from the beginning, had her own agenda, her own plans. That he thought she might change had been his fault, not hers.

He took a deep breath and called once more.

Two glum faces appeared at the railing. Déjà vu, thought Logan. Less than three weeks ago the same scenario had been played out.

He could hardly believe it had been that short a time.

Indeed, he felt as if everything in his life had shifted. As if nothing would be the same anymore.

The girls clumped down the stairs, dejection showing in their every movement. The ache in Logan's chest solidified into anger with Sandra at the girls' sorrow. She had let the twins down, as well.

In silence they left the cabin and got in the van. Low clouds dropped a light rain on them as they left. Appropriate weather, thought Logan, as he made the last curve around the end of the lake.

A few cars were ahead of them, driving slowly, held up by a truck pulling a wide load. Logan tapped the steering wheel, anxious to be gone.

"Look, there's Sandra."

Logan's heart jumped in his chest. He peered through the rain to see where Bethany was pointing.

Sure enough, on the side of the road stood Sandra. Hitchhiking.

The story had come full circle indeed.

"Let's pick her up, okay?" Bethany turned a pleading look to Logan, who wondered at the irony of the predicament.

He bit his lip, considering. Ever since Sandra told him she couldn't come with them, a feeling that something wasn't right had nagged at him. She wasn't being forthright. He made a quick decision. He was going to pick her up. Make her tell him.

"Oh, no. Someone else is going to give her a ride," Brittany called.

Sure enough, a car two vehicles ahead of them pulled over. Sandra picked up her knapsack, slung a duffel bag over her shoulder and started walking toward the car. At the last moment she glanced up, her hair sticking in dark strings to her face. She froze, staring at them.

Did he see sorrow in her face or was he just being optimistic? He stepped on the brake.

But then she looked away, got in the car and closed the door. The car drove away.

"Why didn't she come over?" Bethany said, her voice full of pain.

"I guess she has her own plans," Logan snapped.

He stepped on the gas, swung past the vehicle ahead of them. In seconds he was past the truck carrying a mobile home and in minutes a few miles ahead of the car with Sandra in it.

They would forget her, Logan figured. It would take a little time, but the girls would get over her.

And so would he. So would he.

"I'll see you tomorrow, Sandra."

Sandra waved at her fellow cashier as she walked across the parking lot of the grocery store toward her car. She didn't want to think about tomorrow. About coming back here again. She'd only been working at this job for a month, but she was already tired of it. No staying power, she realized. Couldn't stick with anything. Just like her dad said. Just like Logan had implied.

The thought of Logan made her close her eyes and lean against the car in a moment of weakness. Made her wish that one day she would be able to think of him without experiencing this utter sense of loss. This sense that something wonderful and beautiful had been just out of her reach.

She got into her car and started it. The engine turned over the first time, and she made her way home.

Her apartment was a bachelor suite on the third floor, and by the time she trudged up the stairs and down the hall to the door, she could hear the muffled sound of the phone.

She shoved her key into the lock, the ringing galvanizing her into action. Who would be calling her? she wondered as she finally got the door open. She ran to the phone, jerked it off the hook and sucked in a breath, willing her pounding heart to still.

"Hello," she said slowly. "Sandra here."

"Hey, Sandy, it's Jane."

Funny that her heart, still beating so hard, should plummet so heavily with disappointment. "Hi, Jane." She didn't know why she expected Logan to phone. He didn't even know her phone number. Didn't know where she was staying.

"So how's your cashier job?"

"Tiring, boring, exhausting. But it pays bills." Sandra tucked the phone under her chin as she bent to unlace her running shoes. "I'm getting real good at making change," she said dryly as she kicked off her shoes. She sighed lightly as she sank into a nearby chair, glad to be off her feet.

"Have you considered coming to Calgary to work?"

Sandra bit her lip. "I'm not sure."

"I've got a posting listed here for a job you might be interested in." Jane explained how she pulled it off the bulletin board at the school where she worked as a secretary. "The girl had an accident and won't be coming back. Bad for her, but it might be good for you. I know you're more than qualified for this job, girl."

Sandra hesitated. "I'm not sure, Jane."

"C'mon. Calgary's big enough for you and your father."

Sandra rotated her feet, thinking about going back to a job with no future. A job that paid minimum wage. Too much to die on, not enough to live on. Not on her own.

"I suppose. What's the job?"

"Teacher's aide. And if you get in with this school, I'm pretty sure you could get a teaching job. I know of two teachers who will be quitting in the next year or so."

"Teaching, eh?"

"I know you're thinking about it, Sandra Bachman. From what you told me about those girls, I get the feeling you enjoyed doing that kind of work."

Sandra had connected with Jane when Cora moved out. In no time they had caught up, reestablished their old acquaintence. Sandra had told Jane about Brittany and Bethany. But not about Logan. That still hurt too much.

"I did."

"So why not come down and apply?"

Sandra bit her lip, considering.

"What do you have to lose except a day of work?" Jane insisted.

"I've got a day off coming to me, anyway," Sandra said slowly.

"Think about it. And send in your application, just

in case.'' Jane gave her the address, and Sandra copied it down on the back of a utility bill she had to pay yet. "The money is good, and you can move in with me. That'll save you a few dollars, too.''

"I'll think about it," Sandra said. "It'll mean quitting another job, though."

"Oh, c'mon, Sandra. You have other qualifications. No one would fault you for wanting to use them."

"Maybe." Sandra hesitated. She knew she wasn't using her talents properly. And she also knew that avoiding this job just because she would be using the degree her father paid for was being foolish in the extreme. "But I might not get the job."

"Trust me, Sandra. I know who's been applying. They'll be happy to have you."

"I'll send in my résumé. That's all I'll promise," she said slowly. "Take care, and thanks for calling." Then she hung up the phone.

Supper was quick. She heated leftovers from the day before and ate standing against the counter. She looked out the small window that faced west and another apartment block. Thankfully it was fall and the evenings were cooler. When she first moved in, it was still August, and the apartment was like a stifling oven.

Sandra glanced at her watch and yawned. Too early to go to bed. She wandered into the living room, and with a smile picked up the Bible she had set on the small end table that came with the apartment. She'd been reading it more often lately, finding comfort in the pages that were barely worn. Each time she read it she thought of Logan and his solid faith. Each time she read it she wondered if she would ever see him again.

She unwittingly opened the book to the dedication page. Given to her on the occasion of her high school graduation. From her parents.

Sandra traced her mother's signature, her father's. She missed her mother, but in one way Sandra was glad that her mother had been spared knowing what was happening in Sandra's life. Of course, had her mother still been alive, Sandra wondered if she would have left home.

Still holding the Bible, Sandra dropped onto the couch. She turned to the Psalms. She came to Psalm 103. She read, then stopped at verse twelve. *As far as the east is from the west, so far has he removed our transgressions from us. As a father has compassion on his children, so the Lord has compassion on those who fear him.*

Would her father have compassion? Sandra wondered. If she were to show up on his doorstep, would he let her in?

She fingered the pages as she remembered his final words of anger. Telling her she was ungrateful, irresponsible. That she no longer had a home with him. That she didn't need to come back.

So what if she got this job? Would it prove anything to him? Did she even need to?

Sandra felt a sob slip past her lips. A faint cry that echoed like an empty house. In spite of their angry confrontations, she still loved him.

She bent her head. Covered her face. Then, slowly, haltingly, she began to pray. She'd been doing more of that lately, too. *Give me wisdom,* she prayed. *Show me clearly what I should be doing. Show me how I can fix all the things that are wrong in my life.* She knew what she was doing—working as a cashier—was just another way of putting off what she had to do. She wondered if the phone call from Jane wasn't enough of an indication for her.

She prayed a little longer, praying for her father. Praying for Logan and the girls. It brought them nearer for a moment, and eased her loneliness.

"This is absolutely amazing." Delores Jonserad put down the drawing, shaking her head. "How did you know?"

Logan frowned, trying not to lean forward in the chair he was perched on. "How did I know what?"

"What we really wanted." Delores glanced at her husband, who was staring at the second and third renderings of the house. "Isn't this wonderful, Nathan? Can't you just feel the space?"

"If you want I can give you a visual walk-through on the computer." Logan pulled out his laptop, trying to still the shaking in his fingers. Delores and Nathan Jonserad had chosen three final designs, and Logan's was one of them. He didn't want to look overeager, nor did he want to look unprofessional. So much was riding on this.

Nathan shrugged, laying the papers on the table. "I don't think so."

Logan tried not to let the heaviness of his disappointment show. Having the Jonserads accept his design meant more than just the possibility of more work thrown his way.

He couldn't explain his deep-seated desire to see the

plan he and Sandra had designed come to fruition. It was as if it was the only connection he had with the woman who had walked out of his life two months ago. A woman he hadn't been able to forget.

"I like it the best, anyhow." Ignoring his wife's angry glare, Nathan Jonserad took his pipe out of his pocket and polished it slowly, like an apple, on his shirt. "It doesn't make our house look like a museum. Or Tara. Or Green Gables. Like the others." He winked at his wife and put his pipe away. "I think we'll go with your plan. It has a spark of creativity that I haven't seen in any of the others."

Logan wanted to jump up, to cheer, but instead he satisfied himself with a brief clench of his hands and a quick prayer of thanks. "That's wonderful," he said, smiling at Nathan and Delores. "Just wonderful." He wished he could share this with Sandra. Wished she could be here.

He dismissed the errant thought. He had been thinking about her too much because of this project. Each time he saw the design they had created together, he thought of her.

Someday, he would be able to drive along a city street and not have his heart jump each time he saw a woman with a backpack, long brown hair and a jaunty air. Someday he would not wonder how she was doing and where she was.

Someday, but not yet.

Logan leaned back in his seat, glancing at his watch. He was half an hour early, but he was on his way from a construction site and was done for the day.

He crossed his arms over his chest and opened the window to let some fresh air into the van. It was the end of September, and the weather was still balmy and warm. Fall would come soon enough, he figured, and then winter, bleak and cold.

The thought of spending another winter in the condo with the two girls sent a shiver down his back. He really had to go looking for a house with more room. A place with a front and back door, a yard they could play in on warm days.

A slender figure walking past the van caught his eye. Tall, dark hair.

He tapped his fingers on the steering wheel as he laughed at himself. Of course it wasn't Sandra. Just like the woman he'd seen downtown a week ago wasn't Sandra. Nor was the woman who delivered their mail.

He was doing well. This morning was the last time he had thought of her until now.

Then the woman glanced toward the school, stopping.

Logan's heart thudded against his rib cage, and before he could even think, he was out of the vehicle.

"Sandra?"

Her head spun around, her hand pressed against her chest. She turned, her face pale.

"Hey, Logan," she said slowly.

Logan suppressed a light shiver as his eyes traveled hungrily over her familiar features. There were dozens of questions he wanted answered, but he settled for the common, the inane.

"How've you been?"

"Okay. I've been okay." She hugged herself as if chilled. "I've got a job here in Calgary."

"Doing what?" He wanted to know, yet didn't. Probably some other crazy scheme. Just like his mother.

"I'm a teacher's aide." She laughed, a harsh sound. "Surprise, surprise."

"A teacher's aide," he repeated, surprised at the surge of anger her reply gave him. "That's not much different than being a tutor, is it?"

Sandra looked away, but not before Logan caught the brief flash of pain in her eyes.

He felt immediately contrite. It was really none of his business what she was doing. She had every right to turn down a temporary job in favor of a more permanent one.

"What about your stained glass work?"

Sandra flipped her hair back, avoiding his gaze. "I decided to give that up."

"I see." He shouldn't be surprised. How long had his mother managed to stay with anything? Two months? Three?

Was Sandra any different than his mother, after all? For a time, he had thought she was.

He couldn't forget their last night together. Working on the Jonserad plan. The energy that flowed between them. The ideas that flew around. The vitality she created. Before she left, he sincerely thought something was building between them. Had he been so badly fooled by her?

"So, have you heard from the Jonserads?" she asked, breaking the silence.

Logan's eyes snapped to hers. It was as if she had read his mind. "Yes, I have," he said slowly, still looking into her deep brown eyes. He didn't want to be mesmerized by them. But he couldn't look away. Nor did he want to. "They chose our plan."

As Sandra's smile spread across her face, his carefully constructed defenses melted as easily as frost beneath a morning sun.

"Really?" she said. "That's great. When did this happen?"

"About a week ago."

"That's wonderful."

Silence pushed them apart. Logan knew this would be a good time to say goodbye, but he couldn't help but wonder. "So what brings you to this neighborhood?"

Sandra pulled her jacket closer around herself. "I'm living with my friend Jane. She has an apartment a block from here. I would normally be working now, but we had some problems with the plumbing at school. We got let out early and I...I thought I'd go for a walk."

He remembered telling Sandra the name of the girls' school and wondered if her being here was a coincidence. He decided to push things a little.

"You thought you would go for a walk right past Bethany and Brittany's school."

She looked away, a flush creeping up her neck. "Yes."

"Were you hoping to see them?"

She nodded.

"Why?"

"I just wanted to see them." She tossed her hair, hunched her shoulders. "I wasn't going to talk to them. I just wanted to see them."

"So you haven't forgotten about them."

Sandra's laugh was a choked sound, and she glanced quickly down. "No. Not at all."

Something shifted at her admission. "And what about me?"

Sandra still didn't look up. "Unfair question, Logan Napier."

He wondered if his growing optimism made him imagine the pain in her voice. "Sandra, why did you go?"

"Doesn't matter, Logan."

"That's convenient, Sandra. I offered you a job. I offered you a chance to come back with us."

She looked at him then, her eyes pleading. "I couldn't do it. I know what's important to you."

"And what is important to me?"

"Your faith. Your family. Those two wonderful girls."

Logan nodded. "And what's important to you, Sandra?"

She waited, chewing her lip. "I don't know any more."

She sounded desolate, lost. He didn't know what to say.

"How are the girls doing in school?" she asked, changing the subject.

"They're doing quite well." Logan decided to ease off, surprised that she had already shown him as much as she had. Surprised at his emotional response to her.

"The tutor I hired managed to help them get caught up even though they didn't work as hard for her as they did for you." That was an understatement. The tutor suffered from constantly being compared unfavorably to Sandra and from a decided lack of imagination and ingenuity. Things Sandra had in abundance. "They rewrote some of the exams and managed a conditional pass. So far they're doing just fine." *They miss you,* he wanted to add. *And I do, too.* But he was afraid if he mentioned that, she would leave. Run away. The original free spirit who couldn't commit herself.

So why was she here, hoping to catch a glimpse of the girls? Why was she still interested in what they were doing?

He felt inexplicably jealous of his nieces.

"Well, I should go," she said quietly, darting him a quick glance.

Logan held her eyes, wouldn't look away.

He felt it again. That peculiar connection, an echo of the energy that flowed between them when they were working on the Jonserad project.

He remembered the times he had held her. Kissed her.

He couldn't let her go just yet.

"Sandra, we need to talk."

"What about?" she asked, looking suddenly wary.

Did he dare push her?

Did he dare let her walk away? Did he want to think about her living somewhere nearby and yet unreachable? He had to take a chance.

"Why did you leave?" he asked again. "Why didn't you come back with me and the girls?"

Sandra looked into his eyes, and he caught a flicker of some unreadable emotion in hers. Sadness? Regret?

"I think I have a right to know, Sandra," he continued.

"What do you mean?"

He paused, one corner of his mouth lifting in a wry smile. He decided he had nothing to lose. If after telling her she turned and walked away, he had only suffered a minor humiliation.

But if she stayed... If he explained...

"I thought I'd be able to forget about you, Sandra. But I can't. I thought this would slowly disappear, but seeing you right now, I feel as if any ground I've gained is completely lost. You're occupying too much of my head, girl." His smile faded. "That's the right I claim."

She closed her eyes, lowered her head. "Please don't talk like that, Logan. I don't deserve any of this."

Her words connected with other words, with memories of what she had told him of her father.

He couldn't stop himself from laying his hand on her shoulder, from making a connection to her, however tenuous. "Come and sit in my van," he said. "Talk to me there." He didn't want this discussion to take place out in the open. He preferred the privacy of his vehicle.

"Okay," she whispered.

Logan walked to the passenger door and opened it for her. Sandra, without looking at him, stepped in.

He watched her as he came around the front of the van, then got in. Logan half turned to face her, one arm resting on the steering wheel. He looked at her, wondering where to start.

Sandra shoved her hands in the pockets of her jacket and sighed lightly. "You wanted to know why I left." Sandra leaned back in the seat, staring straight ahead.

"Yes, if you want to tell me," he encouraged gently.

"I left because I know you and the girls deserve better than me."

Logan's first reaction was to negate, to deny what she said. But hadn't he at times felt the same? Yet even as all his previous judgments of her came back to him, one thing was sure. She was Sandra, and he loved her in spite of—and, if he were to be honest, because of—who she was.

"Sandra, look at me."

She slowly turned her head, her dark eyes wary.

He wished he could be as glib as she could be. Wished he had the right words. "Whatever made you think I deserve better than you?"

She looked away again. "My life and how pointless it really was." She laughed, a harsh, bitter sound. "My father was right, and so were you."

"I don't know if I like being spoken of in the same breath as your father."

"I'm sorry," Sandra said. "You're not really like him, but in other ways you both saw who I really was." She sighed, turning her head to him again. "I was just a coward. Just like you said, my whole life after I left home was concentrated around no. I didn't know what I wanted, only what I didn't want."

"You wanted to do stained glass work, didn't you?"

Sandra shrugged. "I'm not sure. I picked it up on

Vancouver Island as something to do. That old work ethic pounded into me by my dad. It paid a few bills here and there.'' She laughed shortly. ''I was lucky I had friends. I thought my big break was that order from the restaurant in Calgary.'' She took a deep breath. ''I never told you how flat broke I was when I first met you. I worked for you only because I needed the money so badly to pay for my glass supplies so I could do the job.''

''Did you finish that job?''

''The company that owned the restaurant was taken over, and the new owners canceled the order.'' She glanced his way again, her mouth curved in a wry smile. ''I found out the day you offered that job to me. Losing that order seemed to underline the total futility of my life. I couldn't seem to do anything on my own.'' She laughed again. ''Even this job I got thanks to my friend Jane.''

''Do you like the work?''

Sandra smiled then. A smile of warmth and humor. A glimpse of the Sandra he had fallen in love with. ''Yes, I do.'' She looked at him, her eyes holding his. ''I also realized I learned something important while I was working for you.''

Logan leaned against the door, surprised at her revelations. Sandra was a proud person. To lose what she saw as her independence was certainly a blow for her. ''And what was that?''

''That I'd been selfish. That the freedom I worshiped was really a way of avoiding responsibility. The responsibility I owed my father for paying for my education.'' She shrugged. ''When I found out I lost the job, I realized what an illusion my independence had been.''

''If you needed work, why didn't you come with me and the girls?''

Sandra fiddled with the zipper pull on her coat. ''Because I was ashamed,'' she said finally. ''Because I felt unworthy of you. Of the girls. My whole life, everything I'd spent all those years developing was proven to be just a sham. A joke. Someone playing at being an adult. Someone who took very good care of herself.'' She blinked, and a bead of silver glimmered in one corner of her eye. She reached up and wiped it away.

Logan wanted to pull her into his arms. To comfort her. But he sensed she had more to say. He wanted to hear it all. To sweep away any misconceptions that had been created.

''I knew of your faith and how sincere it was,'' Sandra continued, her voice thick with emotion. ''I'm still not sure of my own.''

''But it matters, doesn't it?''

Sandra frowned. ''What do you mean?''

''You know God. Yet I sense you hold back, though you were raised in a Christian home.'' This was the true barrier to any relationship they might develop.

''Oh, yes. Mandatory church attendance and expectations and all the rest. But no matter what I did, it was never good enough for Dad. Probably not good enough for God.'' She stopped, giving Logan a wry glance. ''Sorry. That sounded whiny. I made my choices. I have to learn to live with the consequences. But lately God and I have been talking more.''

Logan couldn't stop himself. He took her hands in his, needing a physical connection with her.

He wanted to tell her so much. All the things he had learned. All the truths he had assimilated and made part of his life. *Please, Lord, give me the right words. Let what I say be from You, not my own puny explanations.*

He could see the struggle on her face. And he prayed that she would see the things that God had shown him.

Redemption. The life-changing power of God. The love of a celestial Father Who loved unconditionally.

Chapter Fifteen

"I went to church last Sunday," Sandra murmured, staring at Logan's hands holding hers.

She felt his tighten, but she still didn't want to look up. It was amazing enough to be sitting with him, to have him expressing concern for her spiritual well-being.

It's more than that and you know it.

But Sandra didn't want to entertain that thought.

"And what did you discover?" Logan's voice was warm, encouraging, soothing away the pain she had initially felt in his presence.

"That I'm a pretty unworthy person." She looked at him, forcing a smile. "I've also been reading the Bible more and discovering the same thing."

"Nothing we do can ever be good enough for God," Logan said softly. "But He loves us just the same. While we were sinners, Christ died for us. Not when we were good. When we didn't deserve it. We can never hope to deserve it. It's a gift. An absolute gift, freely given. Surely you know that."

Sandra lowered her head. "I should. But it's not what I saw as I grew up."

"Sandra, your parents' love was imperfect. But God loves you as you are. Yes, He wants you to be better than you are. Yes, He challenges us to step outside of our lives. But not without His help. Not without His Spirit and His love."

His words surrounded her, gently reinforcing the positive message she had heard at church. That He who made the lily, who flung the stars into space, had made Himself weak and vulnerable for the world. For her.

"You know," she replied softly, "it's so much easier to think I'm unworthy."

"Why is that?" His voice was pitched low, creating an intimacy that drew her closer to him.

"That way I don't have any obligations." She dared to look at him, to lose herself in the depths of his warm eyes. "No expectations. That way I could think I was free."

"And were you?"

Sandra shook her head slowly, feeling a freedom in just admitting this to Logan. "No. I was tied down to trying to outrun my father. How betrayed I felt that my mother had died, leaving me alone with him and his expectations."

"And what about God in your life?"

"I think I was trying to outrun Him, too. But I didn't. He found me."

"Sandra, it means so much to me that you can understand this."

She was fascinated by the sight of his hands holding hers, by his comment. "Why?"

Logan's thumbs moved across her knuckles. "Because I've come to care for you more than I've ever cared for anyone else. I thought I could forget you when you left, but I've thought of you every day since you left twelve weeks ago."

"Twelve weeks and two days," Sandra corrected with a light shiver. She looked at him, dared to make yet one more connection with him.

His hands tightened on hers, then he slowly leaned forward and touched his lips lightly to hers.

Sandra's heart spiraled slowly downward as she sat perfectly still, her eyes drifting shut, her hands clenching his.

Logan drew back slightly and rested his forehead against hers with a sigh light as a wish.

"I haven't been able to forget you, Sandra. I haven't stopped praying for you, wondering what you were doing."

Sandra closed her eyes as a single tear slid down her face, cool and wet on her cheek. She wanted to say so much but couldn't articulate the fullness in her heart. The peace she felt stealing over her as if so much had suddenly become right in her world.

"I couldn't forget about you, either."

Logan kissed her again and again, then drew back, still holding her hands, his smile huge. "I love you, Sandra."

Sandra thought her heart couldn't hold any more happiness. Still she couldn't stop herself. "Logan, I don't deserve…"

He laid a light finger on her lips. "I don't, either, okay? None of us do. Love is a gift."

"Then I have a gift for you, too," she said softly. "I've never cared for anyone like I care for you. I love you, too."

Logan pulled her close, holding her tightly. Sandra's thoughts became inarticulate prayers of thanks. He tucked her head under his chin, still holding her. "I never thought this would happen. Not today," he whispered, stroking her head with his chin. "If ever."

Sandra snuggled as close as she could, her free hand tangling in his thick hair. "I didn't, either." It was wonderful, heaven to be in his arms. She never wanted to move.

"I wonder what the girls will have to say about all this," he said quietly.

Sandra laughed, pressing a quick kiss to his warm neck. "I'm sure they'll take all the credit."

"No doubt."

They were quiet a moment. Logan fingered her hair, sending shivers down Sandra's back. She didn't know if her body could possibly contain the happiness that filled her. She wanted to tell him, but couldn't.

So she simply held him, praying he would understand.

"There's something else we need to talk about, Sandra."

"What?" she murmured, fingering the corner of his shirt collar, feeling an absolute freedom in doing so.

"I'd like to meet your father."

Sandra stiffened and almost pulled away, but Logan wouldn't let her go.

"I take it you haven't visited him yet?"

Sandra swallowed at the softly worded question as new sorrow engulfed her. "No, I haven't," she said quietly. "I tried to call him over the summer, but there was no answer. Then, when I got this job, I thought maybe I could tell him that. But I didn't dare." Her laugh was without humor. "I called him a couple of times after I left home, but he hung up on me. I don't know what I would do if that happened again."

"Have you ever thought of seeing him face to face?"

Sandra pulled back, looking at Logan. "If he won't talk to me on the phone, you surely don't think he'll let me in his house?"

Logan cupped her cheek with his hand. "I'd like to meet him. With you."

Sandra lifted a shoulder, pressing his hand against her face. "How can I tell him we're coming?"

"We could just show up at his place. See what happens."

Sandra couldn't repress a shiver.

"I'll be with you, Sandra," Logan said. "You won't be alone."

Sandra blinked as new tears pooled in her eyes at his words. It seemed too much to comprehend all at once.

"I'm not sure I want to do this to me. To you. My father can be pretty intimidating," she said.

"I want to do this for you, Sandra," Logan replied. "I think whether you want to admit it or not, you miss him."

Sandra sighed, brushing away an errant tear. "I do," she whispered.

"Then I'll pray his heart will be softened when he sees his beautiful daughter on his steps, just like mine was when I first saw you."

"It was not," she said.

Logan canted his head to one side, as if studying her. "Yes, it was." He grinned. "But then you started talking. And everything changed." He dropped a light kiss on her mouth. "You talk a lot, you know."

She kissed him back. "Not all the time."

His grin widened. "That's a good thing." He pulled her close and sighed. "'Cause I'd hate to have to compete with you and the twins."

Sandra nestled closer to him, her heart full.

Thank you, Lord, she prayed. *Thank you for your love. Thank you for this man.*

A harsh rap on the window made them pull apart. Sandra felt a guilty flush warm her cheeks.

Two grinning faces were pressed against Logan's window. Brittany and Bethany.

"Well, so much for the quiet," Logan said dryly. "Think we should tell them?"

Sandra smiled as she saw the girls come running around to the passenger side of the van. "Something tells me they already know," she said.

Logan squeezed Sandra's hand and gave her a quick wink. As he reached out to press the doorbell, Sandra felt herself praying. Hard.

She felt like a coward for taking up Logan's offer to come with her, but as she stood waiting for her father to answer the door, she was thankful he was beside her.

Then the door opened, and through it came warmth and light and the gentle strains of classical music.

Sandra felt a clench of sorrow at the sight of the slightly stooped man who stood framed by the door- way, folding his newspaper. It had been five years since she'd seen him. He looked older.

Joshua Bachman frowned and took his glasses off as he looked first at Logan, then Sandra.

Sandra couldn't stop herself from pressing closer to Logan, from clinging tightly to his arm.

"Hi, Dad," she said quietly.

Mr. Bachman straightened, his dark eyes hard. "What are you doing here?"

His voice resonated with anger, but Sandra sensed another note beneath that.

"I live in Calgary now, Dad. I thought I would stop by and say hello."

"After all these years?"

Sandra swallowed a knot of guilty remorse. She'd maintained contact, she reminded herself. She'd written him letters. "I never lived close before."

Josh Bachman laughed shortly and slapped his news- paper against the side of his leg. "No. Your letters came from all over the place. Wandering like a Gypsy. Living off the government."

His eyes ticked over Logan, then back to Sandra as if dismissing him. "What do you want?"

His words were like a slap.

Sandra swallowed the sorrow that began to thicken

her throat. Logan's hand tightened on hers, and she felt another strength.

"I want to talk to you." She faltered, took a praying breath. "I want my father back."

"After all this time?"

"Yes."

Josh Bachman shook his head. "It's too late, Sandra."

"God doesn't think so," Sandra replied.

He stopped then, looking at her. "You turned your back on God when you turned your back on me. 'Honor your father and your mother that your days may be long.'" He paused. "You didn't honor us much, did you, Sandra."

"I tried, Daddy. I did. But God didn't turn His back on me. He kept calling me and calling me. I know I didn't always live the life I should have." She glanced at Logan, who was smiling at her. "But thanks to Logan, I started listening to God. Now I want to make peace with you. I was wrong. In many ways." She didn't add that he was, as well. She realized that was her father's problem, and he would have to deal with it in his own way.

For now the important thing was that she be reconciled with him.

Sandra's father acknowledged Logan for the first time. "Who are you?"

"Dad, this is Logan Napier."

Logan held out his hand, and to Sandra's surprise, her father took it, albeit reluctantly.

"Can we come in, Daddy?"

Mr. Bachman looked at Logan, then at Sandra. Sandra counted her heartbeats as he considered.

"'Children, obey your parents the Lord, for this is right.'" he quoted from Ephesians. "This is the first commandment with a promise, Sandra. And you went against that commandment when you left this house."

"Yes, but the same passage goes on to say, 'Fathers, do not exasperate your children; instead, bring them up in the training and instruction of the Lord,'" Logan said quietly.

Josh Bachman swung his steely gaze on Logan. "Which I did, young man."

"Yes, you did, Daddy," Sandra admitted. She could tell from the set of Logan's jaw this was not going quite how he hoped it would. "And I was wrong to turn away from you."

She paused, hoping, praying that her father's heart would soften. "But you're the only parent I have. And I'm the only family you have. If you don't let me in, we are both going to be even lonelier. I missed you as much as I missed Mom. Maybe I wasn't always the daughter I should have been. I was wrong. I was selfish. But I still love you. And whatever you do right now, that's not going to change."

For the first time since he had opened the door, Mr. Bachman lost some of his regal bearing. He reached out, catching the side of the door.

Sandra didn't know what to do. She looked at Logan.

"He needs you, Sandra," he said quietly.

She knew he was right, and with a quick prayer went

to her father and for the first time in years put her arms around him and held him.

He resisted, almost pulling away from her. But she didn't let go. Couldn't.

Then, with a hoarse cry, he dropped his newspaper and clasped her close.

"I'm so sorry, Daddy. So sorry," Sandra whispered, stroking his head, marveling at the love God had given her to share with this man. Her father's only answer was to hold her, and Sandra wondered why she had waited this long. Then, as she felt Logan's strong hand on her neck, she knew. She needed Logan to encourage her. To help her.

After what seemed a lifetime, Sandra's father drew back, his eyes reflecting a deep sorrow. His gaze flicked over her face. "You look so much like your mother," he said quietly. "I miss her so much."

"I miss her, too," Sandra whispered, touching his hand.

He drew back and pulled himself erect once again. So soon he had drawn his usual barriers of aloofness around him, but Sandra was heartened by their shared moment of togetherness.

"I suppose I should ask you in," he said, some of the starch momentarily coming back.

"We'd love to come in," Logan said, slipping his arm around Sandra's shoulders. "There's a few other things I want to discuss with you, as well."

Mr. Bachman glanced at Logan and then at Sandra. "Well, come in then." He walked away, leaving the door open.

Logan gave Sandra a quick hug, and Sandra leaned

against him, sending up a prayer of thanks for who he was and all he had done for her.

Before they stepped through the door, Logan dropped a light kiss on her forehead. "You're a very special woman, Sandra Bachman," he said quietly.

"And you're a very special man, Logan Napier," she returned.

Then, with Logan beside her, she stepped into her home.

Epilogue

~⌐•

Brittany caught Bethany by the arm. "Sandra and Uncle Logan are going to cut the cake now."

Bethany picked up the long skirt of her pale peach flower-girl dress and ran behind her sister in a most unladylike fashion. She didn't care. Today was an exciting day, and she didn't want to miss a thing.

People stood aside to let them get to the front where the cream layer cake sat in splendor on the snowy tablecloth.

Bethany linked her arm in her sister's, still awestruck with how beautiful Sandra looked. She wore her hair up, tied with a spray of peach and cream-colored roses. Her close-fitting dress had flowing, filmy sleeves that looked like billowing wings. The sleeves had narrow cuffs with shiny beads on them that matched the narrow row of beads at the neckline and the waist of the dress. The skirt was long and just as billowy as the sleeves.

"I still say she looks like an angel," Bethany breathed.

"Except angels don't have brown hair and brown eyes."

"Her eyes look like they're sparkling," Bethany said with a giggle.

"I hope she's not going to cry again." Brittany was talking about the church service, when Sandra walked down the aisle with her father, who looked very serious. Just before Sandra went to Logan, Sandra's dad gave her a quick little kiss. Nothing to cry over, as far as Bethany was concerned.

But Sandra did.

She also cried when Uncle Logan slipped the ring on her finger and then kissed her hand right where the ring was. Bethany thought that was kind of neat, although Brittany was rolling her eyes.

Uncle Logan held up the knife with the ribbon on it.

Bethany had hardly recognized him when he came to the room where they were getting their hair done by Grandma Napier. He never wore such a fancy suit. He called it a penguin suit, but Bethany thought he looked like a movie star. His hair was brushed, and his cheeks were still shiny from shaving.

Now his cheeks were a bit red. Bethany supposed because he and Sandra were having so much fun, laughing and talking to everyone. And kissing each other. A lot.

"Okay, please note that I'm giving Sandra this knife," Uncle Logan announced. "The first test of trust between us as husband and wife."

"Goodness, I'm not about to do any damage with it." Sandra laughed, poking him in the ribs with her elbow.

"Maybe not," Uncle Logan said. "But I don't believe that you can cut that cake in a straight line."

Bethany laughed. Uncle Logan was right. Sandra could never cut anything straight unless it was a piece of glass.

Sandra tilted him a funny grin then looked Bethany's way. Bethany could see her smile change, could see it get softer. She wiggled her finger at both of them.

"C'mon, girls. We're a family now. You've got to help us."

Bethany giggled, and when she and Brittany went over, they were squished between Sandra and Uncle Logan, who had their arms around each other. They all put a hand on the knife and started cutting while lights flashed and people laughed all around them.

Then Sandra's eyes got all shiny, and Uncle Logan reached past the girls.

Brittany and Bethany knew what was coming and scooted out of there just as Uncle Logan pulled Sandra into his arms and gave her a great big kiss.

"When we were trying to get them together, I didn't think there'd be so much kissing," Bethany said with a grimace.

Brittany sighed as she dropped into the nearest empty chair. "But they're married now," she said with a grin. "And it's going to be so nice having Sandra as a mom. Don't you think so?"

Bethany didn't answer. She was looking around the

room. Then Brittany grabbed Bethany's arm. "Look. Sandra's dad is all alone."

Bethany glanced in the direction Brittany was pointing. She could see Sandra's father looking a little bit sad, standing all by himself in a corner.

"He's kind of a funny man, isn't he?" Bethany said, picking up a candy from a dish on the table. She popped it into her mouth. "He doesn't say much and he looks mad a lot."

"I bet Gramma Napier could make him laugh."

Bethany's and Brittany's eyes met. It was as if an electrical charge passed between them.

"Are you thinking what I'm thinking?" Bethany asked, working the candy to the other side of her mouth.

"I think so," Brittany replied.

Bethany jumped off her chair, fluffed up her skirts and started looking around for Gramma Napier.

"Well," Brittany said. "I think we should go with Plan B."

"What's that?"

"I don't know. We'll make it up as we go along."

They giggled and with another quick glance at Logan and Sandra, who were still holding on to each other, still kissing each other, the girls went their separate ways.

They had another job to do.

*   *   *   *   *

Dear Reader,

Just like Sandra in this story, I've always been fascinated by stars and the incomprehensible distances between us and them. We've lain outside, watching the stars, watching meteor showers, staring in awe at the Northern Lights, always overwhelmed and awestruck by the part of God's creation we see only at night. I know God speaks to us through Creation, but it is only part of the Word. The final Word is Christ, the Word made flesh, shown to us through the Bible. I pray that you may experience all aspects of God.

Carolyne Aarsen

P.S. I love to hear from my readers.
My address is: Carolyne Aarsen, Box 114,
Neerlandia, Alberta, Canada, T0G, 1R0.

Next Month From Steeple Hill's

Love Inspired®

LOVE ONE ANOTHER
by *Valerie Hansen*

Romance blooms when Zac Frazier and his little boy move into Tina Braddock's quaint neighborhood. Although the compassionate day-care worker knows the pitfalls of letting anyone get too close, she can't resist extending a helping hand to the dashing single dad and his adorable son. But a heavy-hearted Tina fears that their blossoming relationship will wilt if her shameful secret is ever exposed. Turning to the good Lord for support, Tina can only pray for the inner strength she desperately needs to trust in the power of love....

Don't miss
LOVE ONE ANOTHER
On sale November 2001

Visit us at www.steeplehill.com
LILOA

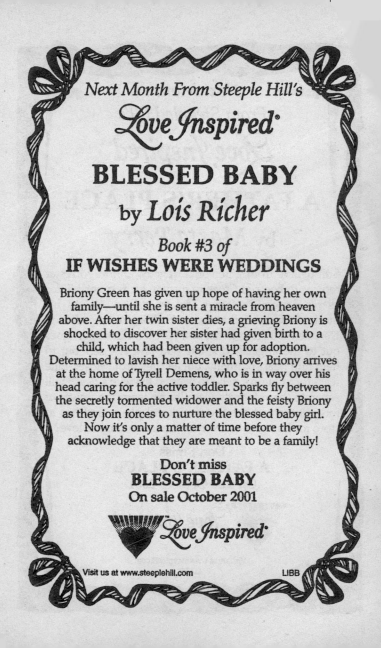